Chocolate

By

Robert L. Putnam

ISBN # 978-0-6151-8378-7

Dedication:

To Don who never failed to encourage me.

To the Young Men of the Los Alamos Ward in Los Alamos, New Mexico.

And most importantly to Steven – my inspiration in all things writing.

Author's Comment

This book is a labor of love. Though the characters and connective tissue between them is fiction, the events and situations in which they find themselves are very real. It has been my sad experience over many years working with youth and young adults both in and out of the Church to have seen, felt, and experienced first hand or vicariously much of what is woven as experiences into this story. I don't apologize for the nature of this work for its very creation has been a healing balm to my soul and to the souls of many of those for whom I give voice herein. It is my prayer that this too will be uplifting to yours. For I know the principles and doctrines included in the telling of this story to be true and of God.

I caution the reader – some events portrayed in this book can be interpreted as offensive by some but I have taken great care to treat such material with the utmost respect and within the bounds of good taste and the standards of the Church of Jesus Christ of Later-Day Saints while revealing the pernicious evil that underlies them for what they truly are. Physical, emotional, and sexual abuse of another is a loathsome practice perpetuated by individuals who, I testify, eventually will be held accountable for their actions if not in this life then in the life to come. If you have been a victim of such abuse, I am truly sorry for your experience and I testify that the Lord, our Savior, Jesus Christ loves you and will share and lift your burden if you only seek him out. I pray that this work will be a healing balm to you as you learn and understand that others have experienced what you have experienced and have survived and been healed to be made whole. I have seen such compassion and love truly change and uplift the lives of those around me who have experienced events such as you will find in this story. If you are now or have been a perpetuator of such abuse I plead with you to get help. The lives and souls that you are destroying are multitudinous, among them - your own.

If you have been fortunate to have not experienced such abuse, I remind you of the following statement that has been attributed to a Prophet of God, Spencer W. Kimball. *"God does notice us, he watches over us, and understands our needs He hears and answers prayers. But it is usually through another that he meets those needs and answers those prayers. Therefore it is vital that we serve one another in the kingdom."* Your compassion and service is often the first salve that can start the healing of a soul torn by abuse. It is not always easy and sometimes exacts a price on your own head. But the reward for paying that price is seeing a life brightened and changed and is truly beyond words or numerical price. It is only something that can be experienced. I pray that you will seek that experience as I have.

I have used, as a unifying thread throughout, a most memorable family home evening taught to me and several of my 12 younger siblings by my beloved mother and father some 30 years ago while in my formative years. I have adapted and modified this lesson on many occasions since to teach the same and similar principles to the youth and young men of the various wards, stakes, and seminaries that I have served and lived in. I do so yet again in this book. Though the concept of one's physical and sexual purity being equated to a prized candy bar seems to be heretical and even to some humorous, I truly pray that you will see and feel the connection as this story unfolds. I know that even today I receive comments and references back from grown adults who, as youth nearly 20 years ago, were taught these principles by my use of this object lesson and have never forgotten it. Recently I found out that one of them has now passed on this lesson to those, like himself many years ago, he is now called upon to teach.

Finally, to all of you that are special to me and for whom I speak in the telling of this tail. I love you, the Lord loves you – pass it on.

1

"Hey, Sheryl. What're you doin'? Looking for Mr. Right?" I called playfully as I walked down the basement hallway of the BYU Wilkinson Student Center toward the lithe form staring up at something pinned to a bulletin board on the wall a few feet ahead. I was heading toward the elevators that would take me upstairs and to the bookstore where I was going to get a few things that I needed for my chemistry classes. I paused near the petit coed that had been nibbling her lower lip a moment earlier as she concentrated on the contents of the bulletin board before her. She turned with a distracted look on her face which seemed to melt into the background as she recognized me.

"Oh, Hi Bill. I might be." She raised her left eyebrow suggestively as she playfully bantered back. "You haven't seen him recently have you?"

"This morning, when I shaved." I replied with a twinkle in my own eye. *Careful, you aren't at your best when you start flirting with the sisters.* I thought to myself. Then playfully, as her eyebrow inched even higher I just as quickly dismissed the thought.

Sheryl laughed lightly and then replied. "Yea, well that all depends on how you spell it doesn't it Brother W-right!"

With a twitch of my own cheek and a lift of my own eyebrow in response, I answered. "I choose whatever spelling fits the situation best."

"I bet you do – in fact, I know you do." Sheryl laughed again warmly and my heart jumped to see her brown eyes flash a little as she shook the silky brown hair out of her face. For a moment our eyes met and then I looked away, my heart already shocked into arrhythmia. *How could you be so bold?* I berated myself even as I embarrassed myself even further by blushing. My mouth went dry and I felt flushed as my heart seemed to project out of my chest. *You're making a fool of yourself!*

I've always been the world's clumsiest male. Every stereotype there is with respect to men being socially inept has begun with me. I'm a chemistry major and, put simply, I'm more comfortable in the laboratory with a beaker in my hand than I am around women in any kind of a social situation. I don't even know what it was that'd caused me to call out to her in the first place. Now, as the reality of what I'd done began to sink in, I was feeling caged and more than a little nervous at the situation I'd found myself in. It isn't something that I would've normally done. Don't get me wrong. I'm not dumb when it comes to girls. I know what they are and I can identify one from a long way off. Like most guys, I can usually talk with them for short periods of time and not put my foot in my mouth but the conversation usually has to be on my terms.

Realizing that I'd gotten myself to the brink of an uncomfortable social abyss here by calling out to Sheryl, I frantically searched for some way to bring things back into my control, to restore the home field advantage if even in the most remote sense. As my flustered mind worked rapidly to come to some comfortable operating condition, I remembered that Sheryl was a student in a chemistry class where I was the student assistant. On occasions I'd taught the class when the professor had been ill or unable to make it to class. I also lead the study and help sessions where I answered the questions that the students had about the homework and study material. My mind gripped this relationship and wrested it into my present situation. *Think of this as a help session. You're just answering some question for her about this week's homework assignment.* I felt myself begin to relax. *I can do this! Yea! This is goin' to work.*

Having decided to use this as my anchor, I looked back up hoping that my face had cooled and wasn't too flustered or that my voice wasn't too fragmented to betray my sudden nervousness and insecurity at talking with a woman. *A beautiful woman.* My own thoughts nearly derailed my fragile bracing for what I knew was to come. One develops a taste for a diet of foot when presented with the opportunity often enough and it seemed that I hadn't had my fill yet today.

Sheryl stood smiling before me leaning slightly against the wall. Her brown, shoulder-length, hair was slightly feathered at the sides. Her high cheek bones and oval face gave her a fairy-like look which was complimented by her petit and distinctly feminine body. Again my thoughts nearly sank me as I began to blush again. *She's got the greatest smile!* As if she hadn't even noticed my embarrassment she continued. "I always liked that about you. It's a good thing that you've got an exceptional spell checker on your computer. I've seen some of your English essays!" She was shaking her head in mock disgust and her hair wafted a fresh washed floral scent in my direction. My knees weakened a little further. To hide this fact I too leaned casually against the wall facing her. She was wearing a pink oxford shirt with a white knit sweater loosely draped over her shoulders a new pair of blue jeans. She had a down coat slung over a backpack at her feet.

"I know." I replied stumbling over my own tongue. "It comes from too many hours in the science lab and not enough in liberal arts." She laughed and then I continued in a little more serious tone as I tried to focus the conversation back onto my own terms. "But joking aside for a moment, it looked as though you were looking for a ride."

It was a couple of weeks before Christmas and school was almost out for the semester. Before I'd called out to her she'd been concentrating on the postings that had been placed on the bulletin board that we now were leaning against. It was the BYU ride board. The ride board had been established years before as a way for students to coordinate transportation to and from school over the holidays or at the end of the school year. I'd used it a couple of times early on as a freshman but now that I had my own car I hadn't thought much about it until I'd seen Sheryl looking at it as I had approached.

The board was separated into several regions based on geographical location in the United States and Canada. A driver that had room in their car for an extra passenger would post a notice on the board in the region that represented the areas that they would drive through searching for other students that needed a ride and would be willing to help pay for the fuel costs.

Sheryl lowered her eyes a little and looked over the top of her books at me as if she was thinking about something. After a few seconds she replied "I was. My car's not feeling very well and I wanted to see if I could hitch a ride before I went and spent money on an airplane ticket. DIA is such a pain to fly into." Sheryl was from Littleton Colorado and my own family had just moved there a little over a year ago. I started to tell her that I could give her a ride but something entirely different came out.

"Yea, I know. Last time I flew into Denver International Airport, the automated luggage system mistook the DEN on my luggage tags for DENmark and I had to wait until Air Copenhagen could return my suitcase. It took four days!" She smiled and my breath caught in my throat as my heart skipped three beats. Alarmed at the boldness of my reply I tried to re-center my thoughts so that I didn't eat too much foot. *Stop it you idiot! You've never been able to joke around with girls. Never successfully.* In my imagination, the delivery had been flawless but as I thought back on what my ears had heard I realized that I was making a fool of myself. A little sobered with the thought, I continued, "Seriously though, when did you need to leave?" hoping that my eagerness wasn't showing through. I really liked Sheryl but I wasn't sure if I was ready to let her know it just yet. I hadn't finished my homework on her. Mind you, I knew where she lived and even had her phone number but I was in a different ward and every time I'd seen her on campus she was with some guy in a polo jacket and turtleneck looking as if he'd just flown in from New England after finishing a photo shoot for some high fashion magazine.

Mr. Turtleneck dressed and acted as though he belonged on some other campus rather than BYU. I imagined him fitting in well with the field hockey players at Princeton, Harvard or Yale, definitely not here at BYU. I knew that I didn't add up to class like that, certainly not if that was what Sheryl was interested in. Still I couldn't pass this opportunity up. If I could get Sheryl to myself for a little while I would be able to tell if I had any chance at all. I'd forgotten all of my earlier thoughts and for some reason felt emboldened. I nearly yelped with excitement as she replied.

"My last final's on Thursday afternoon so I can't leave before then," She said with a slight pout before continuing with obvious frustration. "and everyone on the ride board's leaving Wednesday or early Thursday morning." My heart was racing and every few seconds it felt as though it was jumping the moon. Now was my chance. I'd planned on leaving Thursday morning too but my boss had called looking for someone to cover the afternoon shift. I'd told her that I'd have to think about it and would tell her today when I reported for work.

I worked for an electronics store and with Christmas just a few weeks away the sales of i-pods, digital cameras, gaming computers, and stereos were picking up. Only yesterday I'd made $300 in commissions above my hourly pay. But, working a six hour shift and then driving 500 miles at night wasn't a fun thought, especially if I ended up making the drive alone at this time of year. The weather's usually unpredictable and sometimes turns out to be uncooperative. In the past, I'd even been forced to wait in the mountains for hours while the Colorado Highway Patrol cleaned up an accident or held traffic for the snow plows. *If you wait, you aren't going to get into Denver while there's still sunshine. The ice forms as the sun goes down.* I thought distractedly. *It could get messy.*

As I looked across the few feet that separated us, I dismissed the self imposed cautions altogether. For some reason a frightening new idea began to materialize. I realized that I had my chance to get to know her and talk with her – homework. Eight hours of conversation, just the two of us, while we drove to Colorado together. *You're assuming that you can bring yourself together long enough to hold a intelligible conversation.* My earlier thoughts reasserted themselves. *It'd be a world's record if you could.* Having just thought about it, I decided that if I had to beg my boss to give the shift back to me even after she'd given it to someone else, I would.

"Well - ah - you were looking for Mr Right but would Mr. W-right do?" I stumbled over my tongue trying not to sound too hopeful or nervous. "I've got to work until six Thursday night and I was going to have my car packed and ready to go strait from work." I lied and then paused as I gulped in a big breath to calm myself and then rushed on. "I could pick you up on my way toward Spanish Fork Canyon and the Colorado Rockies."

For a moment I was unsure if my flawed attempt at light banter had been successful or not, it sure felt as though I'd ridden down my grandmother's antique washboard on my tail end. Sheryl just looked at me while chewing on her lip just like she'd been earlier when I first called out to her. Then she reeled me in like a professional angler.

"That'd be great! But, are you sure that there'll be room? I wouldn't want to inconvenience your other passengers." This time there was a little something in her face that told me she was baiting the hook again. I don't know what it was, the slight lift of her cheeks as she said "passengers" or the double flutter of her eyes as she looked up at me, but I realize now that I should've run, before it was too late. I guess that her dark brown eyes and those long, perfectly groomed lashes had been a diversion because I swallowed the lure hook, line, and sinker. I bathed my soul in their chocolate warmth. After what seemed like a century lost in her eyes I shook myself loose, nervously cleared my throat, and then replied as casually as I could.

"No problem at all. I'll pick you up at your house at about six twenty?" A nod indicated that my suggestion was ok with her. I continued. "We can grab a bite to eat on our way out of town. As for passengers, no one wanted to leave that late in the week so I was going to brave the road alone."

It looked as though a couple of hundred pounds had just been lifted off of her shoulders. She breathed a deep sigh of relief which only accented my awareness of her femininity and the small distance that separated us, and then replied. "Great! I'll see you then. I've got to go study for my chemistry final, Dr. Schneider's really tough as you of all people should know." She stooped down, gathered her coat, and then shouldered her backpack and started walking away down the hall. I breathed my own sigh of relief? Satisfaction? Hope!, only to be caught mid breath, choking, as she turned around and asked with the brightest smile I'd yet seen "Do you have my address?"

Coughing over my half-consumed sigh I stammered "I, Uh ... I think I do. Don't you live in the new condos on 9th east?" Then, as if I had to justify myself for knowing where she lived, I lied again, "It's on your registration materials for Dr. Schneider's chemistry class."

"Yeah, number 8." She said with a smile and a further fluttering of her eyes. Then she was gone, leaving me alone in the hall. I let my week knees give in and I slid to the floor wondering at what had just happened. Over and over again I played our conversation out in my mind until I'd convinced myself that what I'd heard was the most polished, flirtatious conversation ever to take place on this earth. Smiling to myself, I stood once more and congratulated myself for being brave enough to finally talk with her.

2

Two, long, agonizing weeks passed as I tried to not be distracted by the upcoming trip. My finals went fairly well. My English creative writing class was a total failure though. We'd had to come up with an original work of fiction, poetry, or pros. All I could come up with was four lines. Three hours and all I had to show for it was four lousy lines. Twenty-eight words of nonsense and it had been agony for me to just to come up with that. I'd been the last person in the class to turn in my exam. Here's what I ended up submitting.

Listen, ever so softly to the word-heavy melody

Of love and peace once known of old.

A symphony of thoughts coursing through

Forgotten threads of divine intelligence.

Pure nonsense right? That's what I thought too. Anyway, hoping to get a better grade if I couched it as a religious experience or poem I titled it *The still small voice* and decided to just live with a failing grade in English. After all, this was BYU. Miracles can happen. When I turned it in at the end of the final I apologized to Professor Freeborn and ran for the door. *So much for being able to get into graduate school* I thought.

Finally, Thursday came and my shift at work was even more hectic than I'd anticipated. Two clients who had purchased new home theater systems that I'd sold earlier in the week came in and while I set those up and tested them out for the buyers, the phone rang off the hook, and some guy who wanted to buy a personal CD player, *honestly – it isn't the 80's!*, dredged the deep recesses of my mind on every little detail that made the Sony better than the Sanyo. All this was happening while snow began falling quietly outside.

I was late getting out of the store because CD man had returned with his wife and wanted me to tell her all the details that made his choice of a player better than all of the rest. Finally, with two inches of snow on the ground and the pace of snowfall increasing, I convinced Mr. and Mrs. CD that the Sony was the best buy for their money, one dollar of which would be my 'commission' for four hours of work trying to sell the stupid thing. Only one thought kept the 'holiday spirit' in me and that was knowing that in a few minutes I'd have Sheryl all to myself for nearly eight hours as we made our way to Denver for the holidays.

As I drove down the hill from the mall toward campus I realized that with every turn of my wheels I was heading home for the holidays. With every block that rolled under my car I recalled the conversation with Sheryl in the hall of the Wilkinson student center. Over the past two weeks of retelling the story in my mind I'd convinced myself that perhaps I could compete with Mr. Turtleneck! I'd made her laugh hadn't I? I could still smell her perfume and the scent of her hair as I closed my eyes waiting for a traffic light to turn green. Lavender - with a touch of sandalwood. Of course, I told myself, I was in denial about just how strong of an impression I'd made on Sheryl. For a moment, I toyed with the idea of stopping at ZCMI and getting myself a turtleneck and imagined myself knocking on her door, dressed in new navy Dockers with a cream cable-knit sweater, a small bunch of flowers in one hand and in the other . . .

"Ah, c'mon you idiot! The light's green. Get a move on!" Even with the radio on and my windows rolled up I could hear the driver behind me yelling and honking his horn. I quickly put my car in gear and, embarrassed at being caught daydreaming, spun my tires in the slush before they caught the pavement and I rocketed away from the intersection.

Reality clicked in as I turned into the parking lot at Sheryl's condo, parked my nine-year-old Toyota Tercel next to a brand-new BMW, and walked up to the door of number 8. Just as I got to within a few feet of the door, it opened and Mr. Turtleneck came out followed by Sheryl. "David! You'd better call! And be careful, I might want to see you again when we get back in January" she said laughing, presumably, from some joke or comment made previously before leaving the apartment. Her eyes glowed happily. Then, on seeing me at her door they seemed to dull and then simply twinkle with a wan

shadow of their previous luster. Sheryl motioned with her head as she took

David's arm and spoke over her shoulder, "Hi Bill, I'm almost ready. Go on in

and keep warm. I'll only be a minute." With that, David led her off the porch

and out to the BMW to see him off.

Crestfallen, I realized that Mr. Turtleneck even had a classy name.

Nothing about Bill ever made one think "What a classy name." Dejectedly I

stepped into Sheryl's apartment and closed the door. I crossed the room and

sat down in a lazy-boy recliner that was shoe-horned into the corner. There I

decided to wait in my misery. *First, it was the CD player and now it's the field hockey*

player. I thought. *This day's been just miserable.* With the snow falling peacefully

outside and promising a rough drive ahead I realized that I had no hope at all. I

spent a few minutes there with my face buried in my hands.

Fully depressed now, I started to get the jitters and couldn't sit still.

For a moment I tried but it seemed as though the few additional seconds that I

sat there was an eternity. Finally, the silence and the depression got the best of

me and I got up and started to pace the floor. As I did so I began to look

around.

A small dusty blue sofa had been placed against the far wall with three

or four decorative pillows piled in the corners. Near the sofa, a telephone stand

held the base to a cordless phone and an answering machine. The message light

was blinking in a steady rhythm that reminded me of the Christmas lights that I was headed home to see. A small end table or cabinet sat to the left of the sofa. The walls had photographs of maple-covered hills in the bright oranges, yellows, and reds of fall, a quaint little fishing village, and a huge poster advertising the Broadway musical "Phantom of the Opera" in New York City. A faint chocolate smell, only hinting of holiday baking, hung in the air as if suspended from the ceiling one calorie at a time and a gold trimmed wall clock hung over the sofa announcing that it was now 6:50 in the evening.

The kitchen was through the living room and contained a butcher-block style table with four chairs. A red candle stood in the midst of a holly wreath decorating the table as a centerpiece along with three envelopes all addressed to other girls, presumably Sheryl's roommates. A white cordless phone matching the base in the other room sat next to the envelopes. The refrigerator was covered with hundreds of magnetic tiles, each with a word or two written on them. It looked as though someone had sneezed a dictionary in that general direction. Moving a little closer I realized that it was some sort of game. Someone had taken a few of the tiles and started to write a poem off to the side.

Silence the dogs of hunger.

Fill the caverns of need.

Escape the refuse of hate.

Discover the voids of pain.

Raise the standard of hope.

Ride the wings of . . .

... It wasn't finished. As I looked for other compositions among the rest of the tiles I wondered if it was Sheryl's work. She was an English major after all. Turning toward the living room I saw a tile off to one side, out of the mess that made up the unknown poet's pond of inspiration. "Peace" Instinctively I reached for it and added it to the last line of the composition. "Ride the wings of peace." Reading the poem once more I nodded. It felt different. *It sounds complete.* I thought. But then again what would I know!

Satisfied and a little more relaxed from moving around, I went back into the living room. A small Christmas tree was decorated and standing in the front corner. Four little teddy bears were positioned under its boughs, each with a name embroidered on its chest, Cindi, Heather, Sheryl, and Connie. Two of the letters on the table had been addressed to Connie. Bright red bows and white popcorn strings complimented the lights, softening the outline of the tree. Small candy canes hung from the branches and an origami angel stood atop the highest bush of needles. A paperback book, splayed open and laying spine up, was perched precariously on the corner of an end table cabinet. *Ten Dollar Dust,* according to its review blurbs on the back cover, was this year's top western offering and was destined to be a best seller. As I settled down into the couch the telephone rang shattering the silence that hung over the house.

Startled a little, I wondered if anyone would come and answer it. It rang a second time and still no one seemed to be coming to answer the phone. I got up, poked my head into the hallway off the kitchen, and asked tentatively "Uh, the telephone's ringing. Do you want *me* to answer it?" No one replied. *Ring.* The third time. I was getting a little nervous since at work we get yelled at if we don't answer the phone by the third ring. It appeared that no one was going to answer it here so I decided that I wouldn't answer it either. It rang again as I started for the door to tell Sheryl that the phone was ringing. As I opened the door I noticed that Mr. Turtleneck (I didn't feel like I wanted to call him David. Turtleneck fit my mood better) hadn't left yet. In fact, he was just ending what appeared to be a draping hug goodby. Sheryl was barely recognizable through the tangle of arms and coats that made up the twosome. Embarrassed to have been a voyeur into a private moment, I closed the door and sat down on the couch as the answering machine picked up the call on the 5th ring.

"Hi! Cindi, Heather, Connie or Sheryl aren't here - we'd love to go out on Friday night but you'll have to ask us in person. Leave us a message and we'll make sure that you get the opportunity. Bye now!" ... Beep

The caller began her message. "Sheryl?" the voice was obviously that of a mature woman, a woman that was more than a little worried. She hesitated a moment and continued "This is mom dear. If you're there honey, please pick up the phone. <pause> Are you there pum'kin?" *Pum'kin?* Somehow this name didn't fit with my vision of who Sheryl was but I figured that Sheryl's mom needed to talk with her so I ran to the kitchen and picked up the telephone.

"Hi, Sheryl's outside right now. Can you hold the line a moment and I'll go get her?"

"Uh . . . Y-Yes." Relief flowed through the headset and onto the floor. Then Sheryl's mom continued a little uncertain now, "W-Who's this?"

"My name's Bill Wright. I live in the Littleton 2nd ward. I'm Sheryl's ride home."

"Oh! Hi Bill, Sheryl told me that she had a ride home with a local boy but she didn't tell me who it was." She paused for a moment and then continued. "I think that I met your mom the other day at a stake relief society meeting. Did you say Sheryl was outside?"

"Yea, she's saying goodbye to Turt – uh - David." As if movement could mask the mistake I had nearly made in referring to David with my derogative nick name. I walked into the living room toward the front door.

"David? Who's David?"

Now it was my turn to be uncertain, "Uh, I . . . uh I'm not quite sure. I only met him a few minutes ago."

"Well then you know just about as much as I do except that I haven't met him yet. Would you mind telling Sheryl that I'm on the phone?"

"Sure. No problem. Just a minute." As I placed the phone on the cabinet next to it's base, I wondered to myself. *Sheryl's mom doesn't know about David! I wonder if this means that David's a new beau. I just might have a chance after all!* Elated with my newfound knowledge I walked to the door confident now that I had a reason to not be embarrassed when I called out to Sheryl and interrupted her goodbyes with David.

I opened the door and quicky poked my head out to see if David was still there. I did so too rapidly to notice that his car was gone and Sheryl'd been just about to open the door herself. I hit my head on hers. Startled, Sheryl jumped back and fell into the snow drift that was forming just to the right of the porch. Stunned by the sharp jolt to the head, I stumbled against the doorframe and in a little bit of a daze looked at Sheryl sitting in the snow. She didn't look very happy.

"Bill, what on earth is going on!"

"I uh I'm oh dear - I'm sorry but the phone rang and I was coming to get you when we butted heads. I apologize. Can I help you get up?"

"I think that under the circumstance that's the least you could do. Who's on the phone?" Her face was contorted into a slight grimace as she brushed snow off of her hands.

"Your mom."

Her grimace deepened and then changed to slight annoyance before she replied. "Oh! Then I don't want to keep her waiting even to trade brains with you, although, I suggest that if we're to do this again, we really aught to have it performed surgically rather than use the brute force method."

Rubbing my head as I reached out to pull her from the snow bank I replied "I agree. I think I'm going to have a headache." Sheryl smiled back at me as she reached for my hand and used it to stand up.

As Sheryl brushed off the snow from her backside and shook the snow clods out of her hair I had a vision. I saw Sheryl running in a back yard somewhere, the snow was falling gently, and two kids were chasing her yelling *"Mommy's go'na be it. We're go'na get you mommy!"* Shaking my head, I mumbled to myself. "I must be going crazy."

"What was that?" Sheryl asked as she stepped into the house squeezing past me and then I stepped in and closed the door.

"Oh nothing" I replied slightly embarrassed that she'd heard me. "I was just mumbling to myself again. I do that periodically."

Sheryl shrugged her shoulders and then glanced around as if looking for something. "Ok, Where is the phone?"

Pointing toward the living room I replied "On the cabinet, near the tree."

She said "Thanks." over her shoulder as she moved toward the telephone.

Wanting to give Sheryl a little privacy, I stepped into the kitchen and sat down at the table. I sat there staring out the window at the gently falling snow as my head began throbbing. A little shaken, I was grateful to be sitting down. As I sat there, the vision came back. It seemed so real. There she was running like an angel in a red ski parka and a blue stocking cap. Laughing and looking like she was having the time of her life. Her cheeks were rosy and tweaked with the cold afternoon air and her brown eyes twinkled when she quickly glanced up at me as the children closed in on her. With a wink she pretended to fall backward into the snow and the twins piled on top of her laughing and crying with joy. *Look daddy. We got mommy. We got mommy!* Then the three of them huddled their heads together as if preparing some sort of devious plan. Breaking their huddle they all looked my direction and with a shout started running after me chanting *It's daddy's turn! Its daddy's turn!*

Laughing unabashedly I played along. We, the four of us, rolled and wrestled in the snow and then, exhausted, I sat down on a small hill next to Sheryl and watched the twins play. After a few minutes, Sheryl turned to me and said *Bill, I've been thinking* . . .

"Bill?"

Startled, I shook my head. Sheryl was standing over me in the kitchen, a look of concern on her face. "Bill, are you ok? I called your name twice from the living room."

"What?" I mumbled, confusion and embarrassment coloring my voice. "Oh I'm sorry. I was just lost in my thoughts as I watched the snow fall." I knew that my face was bright red with a deep blush but what could I do. I most certainly couldn't tell her what I'd really been thinking. *Mommy? Daddy? Twins!*

"Well, my mom wants to talk with you before we go. When you're done, could you just hang up the phone. I'm going to go get my stuff so that we can go."

"Yea, Sure."

Walking slowly into the living room I tried to clear my head. *What's wrong with you Bill! You sure are thinking weird. This makes no sense, one small bump to the head and you go nuts. Clear those cob webs out of your attic while you still have some wits left.* Reaching the telephone I shook my head once more and then hesitantly began speaking. "Hi, this is Bill. Sheryl said that you wanted to talk with me?"

"Yes Bill, I just told Sheryl that the news report is saying that the roads are still open but a little icy in some places. Make sure that you've said a prayer before you leave and make sure that you've got plenty of gas in the car in case you get stuck."

You sound like my mother. I thought. Rolling my eyes at the thought I decided to respond as though she were. "Thanks, I make it a point to never have less than a half tank when I'm traveling at night. That's why I stop for gas every couple of hours." Her breathing seemed to relax and I realized that my conservative approach had been the right one. I continued to elaborate. "Besides I don't like to drive for extended periods of time without walking around a little. Stopping always refreshes me and allows me to loosen up after driving for a couple of hours. If we get delayed at all we'll call. My cell phone number is 412 - . . .."

Sheryl's mom now sighed audibly on the other end of the telephone line. "You're an angel you know that? I was so worried about Sheryl and how she was going to get home but for some reason I feel the Lord telling me that things'll be ok. You're a good boy Bill. Can I call your folks to tell them that you're on the way?"

Shrugging my shoulders a little I decided that it wouldn't hurt so I replied. "Would you mind? I called them from work to tell them I was leaving but that was an hour and a half ago. Their number is 749 ..." Sheryl's mom repeated the number back to me before I continued "I expect that if we get good roads that we'll get into town about three or four tomorrow morning. I'd welcome your thoughts and prayers." There was a momentary pause on the other end while she answered a question from someone else. Then she returned to the telephone.

"Sure. We'll keep you in our prayers. Sheryl's dad wants me to ask you to please come in when you drop Sheryl off. He'd like to meet you."

Why? The logical response jumped unwanted into my thoughts. Out of politeness I answered. "Uh, Ok. Will he be up that early?"

"Yes, he is always up reading his scriptures. Drive safely and pay attention to the news reports. Good bye Bill."

"Good-bye Sister Summerhayes." As I hung up the phone I heard the voices from my vision echoing in my mind, a child's laughing voice cheering. *Its daddy's turn! Its daddy's turn.* After a few seconds a second child joined in. A minute later, I opened the apartment door to help Sheryl out to the car with her luggage. My head was throbbing to the beat of the children's laughter. Sheryl locked the apartment behind us and followed me down the steps as I carried her bags to the parking lot.

The loading of the car went quickly and as I opened the car door for Sheryl I glanced at the sky. Groaning to myself I thought. *It's going to be a long night.* The weather didn't look as though it was going to cooperate. Sheryl got in and out of habit I locked the car door and then closed it before walking around the front to get in on the driver's side.

Sheryl, for some reason, had seemed subdued when she returned to the living room of her apartment with her luggage. I think that she said four words to me as I took her bags to the car and she locked up her apartment. Having stowed her two suitcases in my trunk I'd held the car door open for her. She'd replied with the fifth word, "Thanks." Now we were nearly 30 minutes into the trip and Sheryl hadn't said a single word since then. The drive through Springville toward Spanish Fork Canyon was quiet. Unnervingly quiet. As the snow began to fall in bigger and bigger flakes and the road pavement began to blur into the white background.

Pretending that I was checking my mirrors, I glanced over at her lithe form sitting beside me. With the car's heater working full blast she had taken her coat off and it lay in the back seat. Her eyes twinkled with the reflected light of the oncoming cars but there was something heavy weighing on the mind that was behind them. Her lips were pursed in a most becoming fashion while she absentmindedly twirled a loop of her hair with her fingers. I liked what I was seeing. I liked it even more when I realized that the reason for this sudden increase in my pulse was sitting right next to me and not David. I wanted to say something but I didn't know what I could possibly say that would sound suave and cool. I was at a loss for words so I concentrated on my driving and, being the newly conscientious driver that I'd become, I frequently checked my mirrors. Maybe a little more frequently than I would've normally.

Seeing her there, obviously thinking hard about something, reminded me of the first time I'd met her. I was the assigned teaching assistant for her Chemistry class and Dr. Schneider had needed to go out of town to a scientific conference. He'd asked me to teach the lecture that day and I was nervous, I had never taught a class before, at least not one that lasted fifty minutes. I had a lot of experience leading discussions and making presentations of 15 minutes or so in my other classes but I'd never been in front of 250 students when I was the person speaking. It was intimidating.

The subject material wasn't all that tough though. After all, my favorite part of chemistry was working the equilibrium problems and the topic we were discussing was solubility. Since the solubility of anything is just a function of equilibrium I felt that we could learn a lot just working sample problems on the chalk board. I wasn't prepared to answer so many questions from the students, especially from the really cute girl sitting in the third row to the left of the lecture hall.

I usually sat on the right side of the hall when Professor Schneider was lecturing and so I'd never noticed Sheryl sitting off in the left corner, nor had I noticed that she asked so many questions when Dr. Schneider was teaching. I made a mental note to keep an eye on her.

Two days later she walked into my office the day before the midterm exam with a list full of questions. *"Excuse me. You're Bill, right? You're the TA for Dr. Schneider's chemistry class aren't you?"*

"Yes, I'm Bill Wright." I'd said absentmindedly without looking up from my desk. I'd wondered though, why someone would ask for me using both my given name and my surname. Curiosity got the better of me as I continued my response. *"My office hours begin in five minutes and I need to make a quick phone call..."* I lost my train of thought as I looked up and saw who it was that was standing

there in my office. A little flustered I stumbled back onto the tracks. *"Is ... uh ...*
Is that ok with you? Do you have time to wait for a moment?"

"Yes." She'd replied politely. *"Thank you. May I sit here and study a little?"*
She indicated my officemate's desk.

"Not a problem. He's off at class. Make yourself at home."

Cheryl had waited patiently while I called a colleague at another
university and discussed the results of our joint experiment. The call took
longer than I'd anticipated and 15 minutes later I hung up to find Sheryl sitting
in Paul's desk, her fingers twisting her hair as she looked over an example from
the book. She was obviously trying hard to understand it and failing. After
apologizing for the extent of the wait I sat down next to her and we talked
about science until she had to go to her next class. I don't know if I even
helped her but I do know that sitting next to her, one on one, is what peaked
my interest in getting to know her. It was shortly after this that I looked up her
registration information on her class schedule. She'd been sincere in wanting to
learn as well as in her efforts. Unfortunately the principles of chemistry hadn't
always been clear to her mind.

By the time we reached Price, the snow was clearing but the roads were
still wet with slush. Sheryl hadn't said much of anything now for a little more
than two hours. Oh, there was the time when she'd asked if she could turn the
radio on but when we couldn't tune in anything that we wanted to listen to
she'd turned it off and returned to her thinking. I'd tried to start some

conversation several times but after a few words here and there Sheryl would revert back to her quiet thoughts. I knew that it was going to be a very long night if she didn't at least lighten the mood a little. Besides, the roads hadn't been good coming over the pass and I was tense from the drive and the silence wasn't helping me to relax.

It had already taken nearly an extra hour's travel time to get this far because of the road conditions. To make things worse my head still hurt. I could only see one good thing coming out of the silence. I'd been enjoying my newfound reason to practice defensive driving skills so I had it coming when Sheryl finally spoke.

"Bill?"

"Yes."

"Do you always use your mirrors this much?"

I was embarrassed now and I've never been more thankful for the cover of darkness. Sheryl had caught me in my observations of her. Stuttering I replied. "Ah, I, ah . . . not always b-but the road conditions aren't all that good and I want to be safe."

She looked over at me and, with a stern set to her eyes, replied "I see. We wouldn't want any crazy drivers sneaking up on us now would we." It was obvious that she was trying hard not to smile. For a second her mouth, compressed into a tight line, twitched and then her lips started to curl up. "There are so many on the road you know."

"So many what?" I asked as I looked over at her and became distracted by her dimples as they betrayed the growing smile on her face. My mind was a little confused by her impending smile and the headache didn't help me to focus on what she'd said.

"Crazy drivers." Was her reply with an even more pronounced smile coupled to the tone of laughter in her voice.

My mind was turning to jello now as I lost myself in the conversation and tried to concentrate on the road at the same time. "Th ... that's for sure! I don't think that it'd make the driving any easier if we had to contend with nuts on the road so I was looking for them before they found us."

"I suppose you're right. It's good that you've got these defensive driving skills so that we can avoid the worst of them." This time, as I checked my mirror, she was smirking and our eyes met through the mirror. The warmth of the dark chocolate of her eyes struck deep into my heart reflected through the light of an oncoming car.

With a laugh I began, "Ok, I've been had. I've got to come clean. I was wondering what you'd been thinking about so intently. You've never been so quiet. You always seem to have something to say."

"I do, do I?" I didn't notice the coolness in her voice. "And just how long have you known me Einstein?" This time I did hear the icy bite to her voice.

Stumbling over my tongue I back peddled rapidly. "I didn't mean it that way!" *Idiot! That's all you need to do is offend her.* My thoughts punished me. *You've got at least six more hours of driving. Get her mad at you and you'll never have a chance with her.* Fumbling for some kind of recovery I forged ahead. "I only meant that whenever I've seen you, you've always been so animated and friendly. That time a few months ago when you were in my office for some chemistry help you were so eager to learn and discuss what you were learning that you cheered up my day. Most students simply want to know what the answers are - you wanted to know why the answers were what they were." I swallowed hard before finishing. "What I meant to say is that you brighten a room with your conversation wherever you go but you seem distant tonight for some reason. Why?"

Softening her voice to nearly a whisper she replied "I'm sorry, it's just that my Mom said a few things that've had me on edge and I guess I took offence where none was intended."

I glanced into the mirror again and shrugged my shoulders. "No problem. Listen, my head's still smarting from the bump you gave it . . . " I stopped suddenly at hearing her laughter tinkle like joyful Christmas chimes on Christmas morning.

"I gave it? I seem to recall your bumping into me! Or did I get that wrong?" Her eyes were teasing me now.

"Ok. Ok. I'll own up to it. *I gave it.* But you have to admit that we did bump pretty hard."

"I'll grant you that!" Her hand went to her forehead and brushed her bangs from her eyes. It lingered over her left eye where our heads had hit. "What were you going to say?"

"What I was going to say, before you so beautifully interrupted me with your laughter, - a pleasant interruption mind you - was that I'm going to stop up the road a few miles and top off our gas tank while I buy some Tylenol or something for this headache. Do you mind?"

"No, but are you sure that you're ok? I didn't realize that you were hurt." Sheryl reached out and gently brushed the hair away from above my right eye where we'd hit. I shivered and pulled away a little. Embarrassed, Sheryl crossed her hands in her lap. I wished that I hadn't been so quick to pull away but it had surprised me just how good it'd felt to have her cool and feathery touch brush across my forehead. I shivered again remembering it.

A little embarrassed I said, "I'll be ok. I don't think there's any swelling or anything. To be honest, I think the headache has actually been there since work, but I was so excited about school ending and the prospects of a week at home that I hadn't noticed it until we bumped heads."

She laughed absentmindedly. "I was a little surprised at how hard we did hit. You must've been nearly running when you opened the door."

"Not really. I just knew that your mom was calling long distance and I didn't want to waste her money."

"Well that was thoughtful of you. Thanks." Her voice echoed her actions as she turned toward the window, once again silently looking out into the darkness.

A few more minutes passed as we swam through an increasingly heavy snowfall heading toward my normal fuel stop outside of Price. I'd been stopping there every time I traveled through since I was eight. Dad and I hunted every year in the Book Cliffs to the northeast and this Chevron station was 'our place' where we'd buy our last minute supplies and check our vehicle for mechanical problems prior to venturing out into the wilds of the Utah frontier. The place had grown up with me and had been remodeled a couple of times over the years. The proprietors, Jed and Alice Loveridge, were some of the most special people I knew. They were like grandparents to every weary traveler who came through their store.

When I left home and came out to BYU the year after we moved to Colorado I decided that I'd continue the tradition and stop every time I came through. As I reminisced about good times with my dad I'd forgotten my mirrors for a moment and so I didn't realize that Sheryl was covertly observing me.

3

Bill was an interesting guy. I hadn't noticed, until now, the way his nose crooked to the left slightly, perhaps from a break some time in the past. His ears seemed to jut out of his slightly receding hair. He wasn't beautiful, if I can use that word for a man, like David was but there was a calming ruggedness about him. He was almost handsome in some twisted and delightful way that I couldn't finger. I only knew that there was a little flutter somewhere inside of me when I had seen him in the hallway a few days ago and he had offered me a ride home. Since then, my thoughts had been to some extent on his soft eyes and toothy and somewhat roguish grin. There was something relaxing though about his apparent disregard for things fashionable. He was wearing a long sleeved shirt with a button down collar. One of the buttons was missing and the faded blue of the cloth gave it away as being well used. His faded blue dockers were much the same for wear. I supposed that he wore a tie for work because there was one casually tossed on the console between our seats.

Earlier in the year, in his office, when I'd visited to ask some chemistry questions, I'd noticed his sea green eyes and the slight scar over his left eyebrow. For a moment I thought. *I wonder how he got that?* I almost asked but he seemed to be concentrating on something. His eyes were squinting a little. Instead I looked closer at his profile in the light of the instrument console. The love of life was evident in him from the laughter wrinkles around his eyes and the way his mouth was always slightly turned up at the corners. His brown, moderately-disheveled hair clung to a shrinking protrusion on the front of his forehead and a rooster tail was forming in the center of a shrinking patch at the crown. I knew it was brown from our conversation at the Wilkinson center. For a moment my hand left my lap to brush a stray lock to the side so that it didn't block his eyes. Not that his hair was long or anything, it just looked as though he spent far too much time in the chemistry lab and not enough time in a barber's chair or in front of a mirror.

Just before my arm reached out though, I realized what was happening and as if to hide an ugly mole or something I grabbed my arm and pinned it in my lap with my other hand. Blushing in the dark I glanced over at Bill once again to see if he'd seen my impertinence. He must not have since his eyes seemed to still be focused on something far down the road. I looked through the windshield to see if I could see what it was that had his attention. There was nothing but gently falling snow. A lot of it. Looking back, I noticed a wistful smile had crept onto his face as the headlights of an oncoming car briefly flashed through the window. *I wonder what he's smiling about.*

I'd never noticed the wrinkles around his eyes before the other day at the Wilkinson center. His eyes had been restless at first as if they belonged to a caged animal and then they wrinkled up a little as he tried to jest with me about needing a ride home. His jokes had been corny and he seemed nervous, not like David's would've been.

David was a dream. We'd met in the library in late September. I was looking for an old manuscript for my study of 18th century English poets when I tripped on him. Literally. He'd dropped a book on the floor and was picking it up as I turned the corner, and stepped on his hand while my eyes were focused on the numbering on the stacks. Embarrassed and a little concerned that I'd injured him, I'd offered to take him to the health center to have it looked at. I'd really stomped on it hard. David had only shrugged it off as he massaged the injured appendage with his good hand. *"I haven't had a girl's shoe in my hand since I played the prince in my high school's version of Cinderella. Don't worry about my hand. The memory of such an event is therapeutic enough."*

Smiling warmly I'd replied *"Well then - since it isn't midnight - how about if I at least bought you some ice cream to reduce the swelling your royal highness?"* I was totally amazed at my boldness. I've never been one to approach a guy about a date. Mom said that it wasn't appropriate and for a moment her comments had dripped through my thoughts like a thick oily sludge washing up on a white sandy beach. *A girl that asks a boy out on a date is being too forward. It isn't right. You should make them call you and ask.* I usually questioned that statement but I'd lived by it for too many years to completely ignore her advice. There in the library though, I couldn't help myself. David was just gorgeous and I couldn't help but to just blurt out my invitation.

David had picked up on my light use of humor to hide an invitation and replied in kind. *"Well then, if a peasant girl can afford a few coppers for ice cream the only chivalrous thing to do is to accept, but ..."* He paused dramatically as if he were thinking about what my penance should be. Then he continued. *"Perhaps though, you might consider escorting me to the homecoming dance Friday night instead?"* His grin had been infectious and I found myself agreeing before I even realized what I'd done. I agreed to escort him, that is, if he'd let me make him dinner prior to going to the dance. With a deep and flowery bow he continued. *"Until Friday then, I and my carriage will call for you at 6:30 for dinner and then, if your evil step sisters will allow it, we'll be the talk of the evening, Until the strike of midnight that is."*

Laughing by then I couldn't help but notice the GQ model that was across from me. *I couldn't be so lucky to actually have a date with him, can I?* I'd thought. *He just might be the man of my dreams.* I knew that I must have been dreaming and so it hardly felt strange when I had removed one of my ballet slippers from my backpack and handed it to him. *"Well, since I know my evil step sisters better than you do. Perhaps you'd better take this so that you're not deceived by them when you call on Friday."* Laughing now, he took the slipper and held it dramatically to his heart. After that, we'd talked for a few more minutes and got to know each other a little better. That's where I learned his name, David Colter. I told him where I lived and then I went on looking for the manuscript that had led me to him. All the while a song was dripping through my smiling lips. The words long lost to the joyful and upbeat music that flowed from my humming heart.

Dinner and the Dance that Friday night had been everything I could've imagined and more. David was fluid in motion on the dance floor. We've been dating ever since.

As I looked at Bill one more time and saw the imperfections in his profile I thought *Bill's definitely not David! But at least this time he's my knight in shining armor. I couldn't have afforded to fly home for Christmas and,* as I glanced out the window, *I'm sure glad that I'm not driving in this stuff.* Breaking the silence I said. "Bill, I really appreciate your helping me get home. I know that you'd planned to leave earlier this morning. I talked with your roommate earlier. I'd called to tell you that I was going to be ready nearly and hour earlier than I'd originally thought. He told me that you'd changed your plans. Thanks, I'm really and truthfully grateful that you decided to leave later that you'd planned."

Perhaps I shouldn't have said anything because Bill tensed up for a second and, obviously embarrassed, mumbled something about it being no problem… that he really had needed to work… besides he'd made a few sales today that he wouldn't have made if he hadn't been working. There was something about CD players and his increased commissions from selling them that was in there too. I didn't really catch everything that he said. I was too busy admiring the apparent discomfort on his face and the subtle but nice changes that it made to his profile.

When it sounded as though he was done, I replied. "Well, I wanted you to know that I think it is wonderful of you." I paused and glanced out the window again before continuing. "I hope the weather won't be a problem though. If there's something I can do to help in the drive home, let me know, ok."

Bill checked his mirrors again. He'd been doing that quite often all evening since we'd left Provo I'd called him on it earlier and we'd had a good laugh. He'd been wondering why I'd been so quiet for the first hour of the trip. "Don't worry - we're over the pass and the snow should clear up until we make it to Colorado. There's our first stop." He said as he pointed to a Chevron station a couple of blocks away on the right. "I want to top off the tank and get a couple of snacks. I didn't have time before leaving Provo."

"I'll make you a deal. I'll run in and get the snacks while you pump the gas."

"Sounds fine with me - Could you get me a seven-up and a tin of aspirin?"

"Is your head still bothering you?" I asked as I reached over and, despite my imagined mole, brushed the hair off his forehead as if to examine the slight bump that was there from when he'd used it to knock me into the snow. Bill seemed to relax for a moment and closed his eyes with a big sigh before answering.

"Yes. It isn't bad though. I really am sorry to have been so rough on you. My mom always said my head would get me into trouble someday. Unfortunately it won't be getting me into graduate school. I failed my English final yesterday." There was a deep sadness in his voice as he finished.

As we pulled into the gas station, I almost told him that I'd been in Dr. Freeborn's office this morning returning a book that she'd lent me for my report on English poets when she'd read me a poem that someone had turned in as a final composition in her general education English class. She'd loved it and wanted to know what I thought. When I'd heard her read it, I'd been so moved that I'd had to sit down and think about it. It had been so thought provoking, and even, a little comforting when Dr. Freeborn had read it. Almost as if the "Still small voice", that was the title, were talking to me through that 4-line poem. We'd talked about the poem for 30 minutes before I went to take my last final. Before leaving I'd asked who'd written it. Dr. Freeborn told me. She also told me that she was going to see if this student might like to submit it to a contest that she knew of.

I knew that Bill had passed. *Maybe I'll save that little bit of information for later when the drive requires more conversation.* I thought. Instead I said, "I doubt that. If you can handle English even a tenth as well as you do chemistry then you've got nothing to worry about. It's my chemistry final I'm not so sure about. Would you mind if I ask you a few questions when we get back on the road?"

"No, not at all." He said as he pulled up to a gas pump, parked, and reached into the backseat for our coats. Handing me mine he started to open the door and then paused. "I should warn you though - I sometimes get carried away talking about science so please don't let me make a geek out of myself. I really don't want to turn off that smile of yours now that we have it back on." As if embarrassed he quickly jumped out and picked up the fuel nozzle to begin refueling the car. I was a little stunned. David didn't say things like that. Oh, he flatters me a lot but his flatteries never seem spontaneous like that one had been from Bill. Instead they sometimes even feel calculated and engineered to get me to respond favorably to him. It felt good to hear one that seemed genuine.

A little disturbed at the line of my thoughts I reminded myself again that Bill wasn't David and that David was who I should be thinking about especially after what we'd agreed to in my apartment just before Bill had arrived. Shrugging into my coat, I stepped out and sloshed through the snow to the convenience store inside.

Stomping the snow off of my boots at the entrance as I stepped out of the storm and into the store, I quickly glanced at the check out counter. The older gentleman that seemed to be minding the store was watching a small twelve-inch black and white television propped in the corner of the counter. A little Christmas tree decorated the opposite corner. Green paper holiday garlands hung from the cigarette shelves that completed the cubicle and bracketed the attendant and his life for three more hours until midnight when the store would close. "Ev'n miss." Said the bored attendant without even looking up from the holiday special that had him so enthralled. It looked as though it was some kind of choral concert.

The dust mat on the floor was wet. The muddy water giving the Pepsi logo a charcoal and grey tinge. Smiling at the attendant, I stepped further into the store looking for signs of any other customers. I was alone. Glancing out the window and toward the safety of the car I saw Bill with his head under the hood. *Checking the oil I presume.* Remembering that Bill needed aspirin, I picked up a travel packet of Excedrin and moved on to the drink coolers while I hummed along with the television. *"I'll be home for Christmas. You can... "*

Selecting a 7-up for Bill and root beer for myself, I crossed over to the snacks. A couple of sticks of beef jerky and a bag of peanuts filled my hands as I moved toward the counter to pay for my selections. Setting the sodas on the counter I remembered my telephone conversation with mom and had to grit my teeth again at the frustration that I seem to have every time I talked with her recently.

"Sheryl honey, Who's David? I really wish that you'd let Dad and I know who you've got in your life. I was shocked when that young man answered the phone and told me you were outside with some boy we didn't even know about."

"I know mom, I was going to tell you about David when I got home - it takes too long to say these things on the telephone, not to mention the cost." As an afterthought I'd continued. *"Oh and his name's Bill."*

"Who's Bill? You're confusing me. First David and then Bill. So many young men."

"Using your words 'That young man who answered the phone' is Bill."

"Well then I look forward to meeting him and hearing about David - you haven't forgotten our deal, have you?"

"Mom! For heaven's sake I'm an adult! I can handle myself, you know. I told you I would let you know when I met a new guy I thought was nice and I will. But, does it have to be every time I run into someone on the street or in a class?" I felt a little guilty because I *had* agreed to tell mom about the guys that I was dating and I'd put off telling her about David for nearly three months. I was a little afraid to do so. I felt as though mom would not approve. Now our conversation demonstrated this fact. *"There are sixteen thousand guys out here at BYU. About a third of them are married and don't count. Do you really want me to tell you when I meet the other ten thousand?"*

"Of course not dear but I do worry about you. I want you to be happy like Dad and I are."

"I'll be fine mom - I've got to go now. Bill's ready to load my stuff in the car."

"O.K. Pum'kin. I love you. Please call if there is any kind of trouble or delay and please, can I talk with Bill for a moment?" Her voice hadn't changed. It was still the concerned parent. The same voice that sometimes, like this evening, drove me nuts. *Doesn't she realize that I'm a grown woman?*

"Why? You just talked with him." I was more than a little abrupt with her. She didn't seem to notice. She never did.

"I know dear but I'm sure his mother will be worried and want to know that you guys are leaving. Besides...."

"All right then mom." I said with exasperation. I had to end the conversation before she carried it too far. Knowing from years of experience just what to say I continued. "I love you too. I'll call if we have trouble."

I understand that she's worried about me being off at college by myself. To hear her talk sometimes though, one would think that all she imagines me doing while I'm in Provo is dating one guy after another and never telling her about it. Grabbing a candy bar and placing it with the sodas, I couldn't help but wonder just what it was that my mom had said to Bill.

"Will this be all miss?"

Absentmindedly I nodded as I looked out to the car where Bill was closing the hood and moving around to top off the gas tank. *He seems so....* I couldn't think of the right term. Realizing why I continued the thought. *Mom would just love him.*

"That'll be $4.79 miss."

"What? I'm sorry I was distracted. How much was that?"

"Four seventy-nine miss, unless you want to add that *Snickers* bar to the total." He gestured toward my hand.

"What?" surprised I looked down at my hands and noticed for the first time that I'd picked up another candy bar and was holding it in my fist. Embarrassed I stammered "Y-Yes - please add this on as well as the gasoline."

"Sure 'nough - you and your young man goin' home for the holidays?"

"Who?"

Nodding toward the door it was obvious that he meant Bill who'd finished pumping the gas and was headed into the store. "Him - I remember him an' his dad comin' in every year, ever since he was yea tall to a grass hopper." The grandfatherly figure gestured with his hand to indicate a small child and smiled warmly as he checked the fuel pump indicator on the pump control panel for the price of the gasoline that Bill had put into the car. "It comes to ten forty-eight with the gas"

"Oh," I said, handing him $10.50 and putting the *Snickers* bar into my purse, "we're just traveling together - he had the car and I needed the ride." Just then Bill stepped into the store, a big smile was beaming from ear to ear as he recognized the old man behind the counter.

"Merry Christmas Jed! I didn't get to see you last time I came through in August. How're you feeling?"

Jed seemed to stand a little taller and smiled warmly back at Bill before answering. "A mite bit under the weather but this pretty little lady shore brightened up my evening and made the whole night worthwhile." Jed gestured in my direction. "She reminds me of my own sweet Alice years ago." His eyes glazed a little and the lines of an old pain seemed to creep into the edges. For a moment he seemed lost in his thoughts.

Embarrassed now, I retreated a few steps as Bill stepped forward and took Jed's hand in a warm double hand handshake. "I'm glad to find you in good spirits and looking as healthy as an ox. Dad'll be happy." For a moment a shadow passed over his face as Bill mentioned his father. Then in a more personal and concerned voice he continued, "How's Alice doing?"

Clearly Jed was touched by Bill's inquiry as a hint of a tear formed in his eye and his chin quivered. The memories he'd been cataloguing seemed to catch up with him and his eyes registered a deep pain. The television had been forgotten long ago. "Alice, bless her heart, fought the fight but the good Lord took her home in July. She'd been hurtin' som'pin fierce and it tore me up to not be able to 'elp her. I 'spect it won't be long before I'll be wi' her again."

A small tear tore at the fabric of Bills eyelids as he swallowed hard before squeezing Jed's hand again tightly and saying in nearly a whisper, his voice clearly full of deep emotion. "I didn't know or I'd have been here. I'm sorry. I'll miss her though." After a short pause while he swallowed again, Bill continued with his voice cracking with pent up emotion. "She was the one that sold me my first can of worms back when Dad and I went fishing down to lake Powell. All I had was a nickel and the worms were a dime. I was near tears when I realized that I couldn't afford them." His eyes softened even further and a small tickle of tears began to roll down his cheeks as he smiled retrospectively before finishing. "She saw my disappointment and with a smile so big it must have hurt her mouth she told me that I could have the worms for a nickel if I could help her with something that needed doing. She wanted me to think that I was working off the extra nickle." Bill chuckled a little as he remembered. Even with the tears in his eyes. "It was years later that it dawned on me that I couldn't possibly have been helping her by eating the extra ice cream bar that wouldn't fit in the ice cream cooler. All I remember is that I got my worms and it was the best thing that anyone ever did for me." For a moment Bill closed his eyes tightly and seemed to battle something deep inside of himself.

With tears in his eyes Jed smiled back - "That was my Alice. I only started makin' a profit on my ice cream this summer." Jed reached across the counter to clap Bill on the shoulder. "I haven't seen your dad lately. How's he doing?"

Bill seemed to loose the battle as his shoulders drooped and the tears welled up even stronger. "He ... He had a stroke last summer. He doesn't remember ..." Bill's head dropped to his chest as his shoulders rocked in anguish. Jed came around the counter to enfold Bill in his arms where Bill nearly collapsed whispering. "He doesn't remember our time together. It's all gone."

Jed took a few moments to just cradle Bill's head on his shoulder as he whispered a few things into his hair. I seemed to have been forgotten. For a moment, time stood still and I stood observing something that I could only describe, and inadequately at that, as sacred. I wanted to be able to say something and comfort the two men standing before me but I couldn't find the words. Instead my thoughts intruded. *This is a new side of Bill.* It was comforting to see two men, two friends, secure in their selves enough to cry on each other's shoulders and comfort one another.

After a few minutes, Bill regained his composure and pushed back from Jed's embrace. He looked around self-consciously before seeing me and turning red with embarrassment. "Sorry, I thought I'd gotten over it." Our eyes met for a moment and I found myself wishing that I could give him a hug and I longed to be the one to tell him that everything was going to be all right. Instead, I nodded almost imperceptively as if to tell him that I didn't think less of him in the slightest. He nodded back, he'd understood our unspoken exchange.

Jed recovered next and began steering Bill toward me with his arm. When the two had joined me at the front door Jed gave Bill a quick hug. Silent but dripping with love and emotion Jed pushed us both toward the door. "Bill, you've got 'im for eternity jus' like I 'ave my Alice. Be happy for that. Christ did that for us. This is his season. You have a merry Christmas and that goes for you too Miss..."

A little startled by Jed's addressing me it took me a moment to fill in the blank. "Summerhayes"

" ... Miss Summerhayes, your being here reminds me of all that was good in my dear wife. She had your hair you know. For some reason I don't miss her nearly as much as I was a few minutes ago. You take care of this boy now. My Alice can't do it anymore, Merry Christmas Bill. God bless you both."

"Merry Christmas to you too Jed." The earlier breakdown in his voice and emotions seemed to have been repaired. "I hope I'll see you when I come back through on my way back to Provo."

As Bill and I left the store, I was wondering what kind of woman Alice had been that she would make lasting friends out of strangers that she met. People like Bill and his father. The wind had picked up and the snow was blowing around making the weather look even fiercer than it probably was. As I stepped into the slush of the parking area to go back to the car I glanced back into the store at Jed. He stood by the door watching us as we walked away. I lifted my hand in a wave good bye only to see him wipe a small tear from his eye and wave back with a big smile. I realized that Jed was just like Alice. I'd just made a friend that I'd cherish forever and ten minutes ago he'd been a complete stranger. Brushing a small tear or snowflake, I'm not sure which it was, from my own face I took Bill's arm for support as we walked together through the slush and snow back to the car.

The storm seemed to be thinning out as we merged into traffic on highway six, out of Price heading toward the interchange with interstate 70. Bill was wiping his eyes surreptitiously and didn't say much for the first twenty minutes. I sensed that he needed more time to cycle his grief. He'd lost a great friend and needed to be alone with the pain. That pain had wounded him yet again as it reminded him of what he'd lost in his father. As I waited for Bill to break the silence on his own I remembered a night a few weeks ago when David and I'd been walking around in the mall and noticed a young child that was crying.

"Look at that little boy. He looks lost."

"Yea he does. Someone'll be along shortly to help him. I'm sure."

Astonished I'd looked at David to see if he'd been joking. His eyes had already left the little boy and moved toward the Gap as he started to pull me toward the sales racks. A little frustrated I'd said *"Why don't we see what we can do to help."*

David had callously replied *"He isn't hurt or being abducted so why should we interfere. We've got to be back for family-home-evening in ten minutes and I wanted to look at these jeans that are on sale. Besides someone would just think we're the reason he was upset.*" As I was about to say something in response, I noticed that someone, a woman, was rushing to the little boy's aid. David had noticed too. *"Look, there's his mother anyway. It's amazing that someone could loose their kid that way. I'd never do that and,"* he'd given my hand a suggestive little squeeze *"I would hope that when I get married, my wife wouldn't either."*

I'd been bothered by David's apparent callousness but he'd been right - we'd have been late for family-home-evening and things had turned out fine for the little boy. Instead of saying anything I proceeded to follow David as he found a new pair of jeans. We went to family-home-evening a few minutes later with me only feeling slightly guilty at not helping the little boy.

Now, after meeting Jed and seeing what kind of a bond he and his wife had formed with a complete stranger some years ago, I felt even more ill at ease for listening to David at the mall and letting him lead me away from a child that was indeed needing comfort.

For a moment I pictured a small toe-haired boy with an oversized fishing cap rocking precariously on his head. The hat was held on only by mis-proportioned ears that jetted from the side of his head. A nickel was clutched in his hand as he stared at a tub of worms and imagined the whale that he'd catch with his dad later that day. Then, as he presented his proposed bait at the counter with his savings in hand, I imagined his disappointment when he didn't have enough to purchase the much needed worms. I watched in my mind's eye as the sparkle in his dimmed and the fish swam away in the droplets falling from his cheeks. With resolution he proceeded to take the tub back to its place on the shelves. Placing it reverently back in its rightful place - rotating it until the label could be read by the next angler needing bait. Quietly, wiping another tear from his eye, he turned to leave, his head drooped in sorrow.

Suddenly, from out of no where, an older woman appeared. The sun was glaring through the window behind her. Her head was wreathed in a warm yellow glow as she knelt on the floor near the boy and put an arm around him whispering quietly in his ear. Slowly the tears stopped and a smile broke onto his forlorn face. Soon his head bobbed up and down and the fisherman embroidered on the hat seemed to turn green with motion sickness as his ship bobbed in rhythm with the young man's eagerness.

I watched as the boy's father entered the store, paid for his gas, and, with the boy proudly traipsing after him, returned to his car. As the duo drove away, the young Captain Ahab, grinned broadly and waved a half eaten ice cream bar while clutching a can of worms. The woman smiled to a man shelving bags of charcoal briquets who winked back at her as he smiled back and then shrugged his shoulders. She then turned back to help another customer with their purchase while she casually fingered the precious nickle that was new in her hand.

Wiping a tear from my eye I decided that next time I saw a little child in need. I'd not let my opportunity pass me by. I'd live up to the expectations that Jed had of me. After all, David's a big boy and can pick out his own clothes. He doesn't need my permission.

Preoccupied with my thoughts I didn't realize that Bill had spoken. "…chemistry question?"

"What?" I said in confusion.

"You said you had a chemistry question." Bill repeated.

"Oh, yea! I'm sorry." I was embarrassed to have been caught daydreaming so I quickly pulled my mind in from the fishing spot where it'd been moored and remembered the problem that I'd had with my chemistry final. "I was a little confused, on my final examination about the oxidation state of iron in ferric oxide? I always seem to get mixed up when it comes to figuring out oxidation states."

"Three." Bill replied quickly.

"Three what?"

"Its three. The oxidation state of iron in ferric oxide is three."

"How do you know?" I asked with more than a little frustration. *Why can't I understand this.* I thought.

"Well, oxygen's always minus two" Bill paused momentarily and then absentmindedly continued. "except when you have a peroxide and then it's minus one. Anyway since there are three oxygen atoms in Fe_2O_3 (he said it as ' ef-ee-two-oh-three) there's a total of minus six charge. The material has to charge balance so there must be a plus six charge shared by the ef-ees, the iron. With two to share the charge they each must have a plus three oxidation state."

"Why can't it be plus two and plus four? That makes six." I asked honestly confused. Wasn't that just as logical of a conclusion?

Bill shrugged his shoulders and replied. "The rule is that they've got to share equally, if at all possible."

I was flustered. "I still don't think that I understand it." I said forcefully.

Bill paused and then after thinking for a moment continued. "Well, let's see. Assume that you've got something like salt, (en-aye-see-el), sodium chlor… " My mind filled in the chemical formula, NaCl, before it went blank.

Five minutes later Bill asked. "Do you understand it now?"

"Hmm?! Oh, yea, I think so." I hurried to cover the fact that my mind had wondered and I hadn't really understood a thing. "How is it that you can remember all of the rules and stuff that chemistry seems to have?"

Again Bill just shrugged. "I don't really see them as difficult to remember. They all link together and are logical. Remembering one or two allows me to derive the others using the basic principles of chemistry and physical law. It's not like English where there are exceptions to every rule. Most chemistry rules have no exceptions."

Feeling a little defensive I responded emphatically. "English isn't all that bad though. Once you understand what's going on and what good grammar is, the rest just comes naturally."

Bill laughed lightly. "Not for me, it doesn't. I guess we're both students of the right discipline. English seems so easy for you and chemistry just seems natural to me."

Realizing we weren't in any kind of competition I chuckled as well. "I guess you're right. Thanks for the help anyway." Glancing out the front window I quickly added. "How's the road?" The storm seemed to have disappeared and there was just a little blowing snow.

"Dry - thankfully." Bill paused. "We're in the middle of a desert though, and it's always dry here. I'm a little worried about the Colorado passes though."

"Where's your next stop usually?"

"Grand Junction. I usually get good enough mileage so that if I gas there then I can make it the rest of the way home on a full tank. It's so expensive to get gas at the ski resort towns."

"Do you need a break at all? I mean I could drive for you a little and you could rest."

Bill seemed relieved that I'd offered. "Actually, If you don't mind, I think it might not be a bad idea. I'm not sleepy at all but it's safer if I don't try and push myself. It was a long day at work."

"Well - pull over next chance you get and I'll spell you at the wheel."

"Thanks"

It didn't seem as though it was more than five minutes later that we reached the interstate. Bill pulled off the road a little and we switched places. I had to move the seat forward a little. I hadn't noticed that Bill was so tall. Over the next hour or so we talked about school and what our future plans were. I wanted to get Bill to talk about his father with me. I wanted to understand him better. But that topic seemed to be closed.

Bill wanted to eventually go to graduate school in chemistry. He hadn't decided where or what field of chemistry he wanted to specialize in though. I, on the other hand, really hadn't made any plans past getting my degree. In all honesty I'd started BYU thinking like my mother that I'd get my degree and meet my husband. Now, with only a semester left before I graduated, I was a little confused as to what I wanted to do, obviously I hadn't met my husband yet and I was starting to see a bigger world. I wanted to do something substantial after I graduated. I just didn't know what that would be. Bill didn't say anything though. He sincerely seemed to want to listen and hear my plans. David on the other hand had quickly pointed out *"You don't need to plan for anything after you graduate. You'll get married and start a family. You can't work then."* I was getting a little scared.

The more time I spent with Bill the less I was comfortable with what I saw in David. This wasn't supposed to happen. Not after David and I had started talking about marriage. I was getting confused but for some reason I was happy being with Bill. He seemed so honest and sincere, different from David. For a moment, I looked over at him sitting there with his eyes closed waiting for the aspirin to take effect, and I wondered what it was about me that made me want to find out what it was like to be near him and to hold his hand.

4

When Sheryl offered to take over the driving, I was relieved. The muscles in my neck were cramping up from tension caused by the poor driving conditions earlier as we came over the pass from Spanish Fork. The aspirin hadn't yet taken care of my headache and I was also a little worried about the Colorado portion of the trip. While Sheryl was in the store, I'd been listening to the radio and the forecast wasn't good. We were going to get more snow and the storm was moving east with us. I knew it was going to be a long night. Sheryl's taking over the driving while the conditions were good was an answer to a private prayer begun shortly after getting back on the road.

As we rolled toward the state line, I leaned my seat back and closed my eyes silently willing the aspirin to work quicker. Sheryl seemed to understand that I needed the time to my self. Jed's news had been a surprise to me. My reaction to his news had been a shock. Since my Dad's stroke six months ago I'd resigned myself to the fact that I at least could remember our times together. I could still hear his vice in my mind as he bore his testimony about the creation and pointed out all the beauty around us as we hunted and fished together. I had been growing up at that time. I'm a product of his faith and example.

Because of that, I too knew that one day we'd be together and his memory would be restored.

Besides I'd told myself. *It isn't as though he is dead, I can make new memories with him.* This had all been a mental exercise for me, one that seemed to break down when I learned from Jed about Alice's death. It wasn't until then that I realized emotionally that I still had a problem with my emotions.

I was embarrassed. Sheryl had seen my reaction. I'd cried like a baby. I was a grown man and I'd humiliated myself in front of her. It didn't matter that she didn't seem to be bothered by my outburst it was still embarrassing and the shame of it made my reaction all that more troublesome.

Since she took on the driving she'd tried to start a conversation about my family. But I knew that she was simply probing me about Dad. I begged off using my headache as an excuse. Eventually she fell silent for a while and I had time to think. When I did, I realized that Jed was right on one thing. Sheryl reminded me of Alice too.

I decided that I needed to get to know her better. If that meant that I had to open up to her then I'd do that but I wasn't sure how. I'd already silenced her casual inquiries. I wanted to know her better. In fact, I wanted her to know me better. I felt awkward though. I wasn't sure what to say that would not make me sound like the geek I was. I was still a little upset with myself for my impromptu lecture on oxidation states. I'd noticed that Sheryl seemed to zone out on me. I just don't know when to stop talking about something that's interesting to me. Several minutes later Sheryl broke the ice for me, and I sighed with the release of the tension that had been building in me.

"Bill, you served a mission didn't you?" Her question was tentative as though she wasn't sure if she was intruding on my thoughts or not.

I decided to let her know that I was ready to talk. "Yea - I went to Arizona, why."

She exhaled as though she had been holding her breath waiting to see if I would respond. "What was it like? I've been thinking that I might like to go on a mission after I graduate."

My first thought was *Great! If she's thinking about a mission then she's not serious about David.* Then I listened to the emotions in her voice. *She really means this. Don't capitalize on it like a vulture.* "I think that would be a great idea, some of the most effective missionaries we had were the Sisters. As for my mission, I really loved it. I spent some time on the Indian reservations and really learned to love the Lamanites. You know some scientist has been studying the genetic history of the Native Americans and the native populations of central and South America. He's determined that as many as 85% of the men can trace their genes back to one man.[1]" Realizing that I was starting to lecture again I quickly wrapped it up by bearing my testimony. "If I didn't already know that the *Book*

---

[1] *Science* 1999, 283, pp. 1439-1440.

of Mormon was true I could almost believe that the Lehi story could be true, just based on science."

"That's interesting." She paused as if thinking about what I'd said. Then she continued. "You really love science don't you?"

"Yea, I guess I do but, I already know that I've talked too much science for one night." I frowned absentmindedly.

"What do you mean?" She asked, looking over at me.

"Well" I shrugged my shoulders and gestured toward her. "I could give you a quiz on oxidation states if you'd like me to." Suddenly she burst out laughing. Not a strained little giggle but the full throated tinkle of merriment that I'd heard when she was with David. My hope surged. I'd made her laugh.

Sheryl momentarily let go of the steering wheel and raised them over her head as though she were surrendering in battle. "Guilty as charged" She returned her hands to the wheel and looked over at me. "Sorry, I just can't seem to school myself to concentrate on science. My Science classes were my worst classes in high school and I'd probably not take any more of them if I didn't have to do so to fulfill my general education." She sighed. "Even so I waited to take it until my senior year secretly hoping that they'd change the graduation requirements. No such luck."

I chuckled. "Well I should be apologizing - I started lecturing - one of my weaknesses. Forgive me?" I said trying to look as meek and contrite as I possibly could. Sheryl obviously was having fun now, whatever had been bothering her earlier seemed to have been resolved or forgotten. She'd obviously forgotten or forgiven my earlier silence as well.

Shaking her finger at me as if to scold me she said "Just don't let it happen again young man. I don't want to have to send you to bed without your supper." Her eyes momentarily reflected the light from an oncoming car as she looked over at me with a pout on her face that was quickly falling apart into a full toothed grin.

"Yes mother." I replied timidly.

For some reason she reached over and patted my hand playfully "That's ok son. We still love you even if you did do something wrong. You can always repent. You know." She didn't move her hand back to the wheel though. She let it rest there on the console between our seats. The energy radiating from it seemed to embolden me and I stuttered out a question as if I were a scared child. At the same time I reached over and grabbed her hand as though I needed comfort.

"M-Mom, w-when is it going to be light out? I'm scared that the snow monsters are going to come and get me." Then, still in a child's voice but timbered with the solid wisdom of a child that had figured out the answer, I continued.. "The sun melts them. You know." Sheryl squeezed my hand and continued on with my little game as though she were my mother.

"In a little while Billy. Did you say your prayers? Heavenly Father can keep you safe from the snow monsters."

Her comment was like a gut punch, and for a moment I jerked at remembering my promise to her mom. To cover myself I replied. "Actually, I forgot, could you help me? I don't want to get eaten by a snow monster. They have big cold icicle teeth." The truth was, I *had* forgotten. I always had a prayer when I was traveling. It was kind of a family tradition and I had continued it when I went off to school. As much as I didn't want to let go of Sheryl's hand I gave it a little caress with my thumb and continued. "Seriously - I usually do say a prayer when I'm traveling and I forgot to say one before we left even though I promised your mom that we would. You wouldn't mind if we were to say one now would you? Better late than never don't you think?" I let go of her hand as I started to fold my arms.

Sheryl looked at her mirrors and then over her shoulder as though she were going to pull over to the side of the road. "Actually, I'd feel better if we did. Do you want me to pull over so that we can say one?"

Glancing out at the road I saw the snow piled up on the side. I decided it wasn't such a good idea to pull over. "No - I'll just say one while you drive. We probably better keep on the road. The snow's starting to pile up on the side there and who knows - we might get stuck if we stop." As an after thought I continued with a little wink. "I also think that Heavenly Father'll understand if you don't close your eyes." Sheryl's reply took me off guard a little. Was she playing along with the earlier game and reacting to my wink or was she serious in her reply?

"O.K. but would you hold my hand for the prayer" She blushed a little. I could barely see it by the light of an oncoming car. "In my family we always hold hands when we have family prayer."

Recovering quickly, I happily reached over and took her hand in mine. Giving it a gentle squeeze, I answered as though our game was still on. "Sure mom. Anything you want." I said a prayer asking Heavenly Father to help us to get home safely. After the prayer Sheryl didn't let go of my hand and I decided not to remind her that we were still holding hands even before our first date. Instead I began congratulating myself. *After a rough start this trip isn't turning out so bad, almost the heaven that I'd imagined. Now if the weather'll hold I'd feel a little better.* Even as I was thinking, I was hearing children's voices again. *"It's my turn to be next to dad! Mom always gets to hold his hand when we have prayer."*

After a few moments I spoke, hoping that my voice would not crack in my nervousness at holding Sheryl's hand. "Sheryl, what are your plans after you graduate? You mentioned a mission."

"I really don't know. She sounded frustrated. "I've thought of going into journalism or writing for a living. I've had a few things published so far, mostly little poems or a short story here or there. I want to go on a mission but I'm not sure if it is right for me. You know what I mean don't you?"

"You mean the advice from President Hinkley on sisters and missions?"

"Yea, I know that I don't have the obligation to go like you did but I still feel that I could learn and strengthen my testimony a lot if I did go. Besides, I like the idea of being a returned missionary. I like the sound of it."

"I think you'd make a great missionary." I said sincerely.

"Really? What makes you say that? You don't really know me all that well." She glanced over at me as she changed lanes to pass a tanker truck that was lumbering away.

As I started to answer, I had to tell myself to slow down and think about what I was saying. *She's right. As far as she knows you don't know very much about her.* "Well, you seem to be sincere when it comes to the gospel. The other day in Sunday School you taught a great lesson on being a friend. If you're half as good of a missionary as you were a teacher you'll do just fine." I was a little late realizing that I'd gone too far. After all we weren't in the same ward so I shouldn't have been going to her Sunday school class.

Looking directly at me now, Sheryl asked, "Why were you in my Sunday school class? You weren't spying on me were you?" The right side of her mouth lifted as though she wanted to smile but was trying to hide it.

Oops! Now you flipped. I yelled at myself. *Lets see you get out of this one.* "Well, I uh ... I.... I did check out your ward the other day." *Honesty is a good start.* "I'd gone to the lab to check on an experiment that I was running through the weekend. It required regular monitoring every six to eight hours. As a result I was about 45 minutes early for my own ward when I saw you carry your books into a classroom." *And the black velvet dress you were wearing was sensational.* I faltered. *Stop it! This is hard enough without complicating things. Stick to the subject.* "I just followed the crowd and sat in the back. I hope that I haven't embarrassed you like I have myself." Once again this evening I found myself thankful for the darkness. I knew that I was blushing and stammering like a newly ordained teacher at his first stake dance.

Clearly she was a little confused but it appeared to be pleasantly so because I could feel her pulse quicken under my fingers and she had to take a few deep breaths before she replied. "I guess that I can't be upset. In fact I'm a little flattered. I remember that lesson. It was on the parable of the Good Samaritan and had come at a particularly germane time in my life. I'd just discovered something about myself that I didn't feel comfortable with and I really felt that the lesson applied to me." She paused retrospectively before continuing in a whisper. "I wanted to teach it in a way that I would understand it and feel its importance as if I were the student and not the instructor."

"What do you mean?" I asked. "I remember you bore a really moving testimony on the importance of helping those around us that are in need, particularly those that can't help themselves."

She frowned momentarily before answering. "I'd been reminded earlier that week that I wasn't a good Samaritan when I'd gone shopping with David and we'd seen a little boy crying because he was lost. We didn't stop to help him and I'd been bothered by that for several days." My hand tensed at the mention of David and I know that Sheryl noticed it too because her eyes quickly glanced over at the console where our hands were clasped together. The fingers interlocked. Then they politely returned to the road. "I'm glad that it was my turn to teach that Sunday. It taught me just how much further I really have yet to go to become like my Father in Heaven." She didn't say anything more about David but I suddenly became very self-conscious of my sweaty palms and clammy grip. Still, it wasn't until we pulled into the gas station in Grand Junction ten minutes later that she let go of my hand.

"Is this place ok for getting gas?"

"I always stop here anyway so, of course." I replied glancing at my watch and then continuing "Its getting late, it's nearly one thirty. Let's ask about the weather ahead. Then, perhaps we should call our parents and let them know when we think we'll get in. I know my mom's still up this late at least." *Dad goes to bed early now, ever since the stroke.* I thought. *Mom thinks it's a result of his medication.*

"That's probably a good idea. Why don't you go call and I'll put the gas in this time?" Her reply had been a little more formal than I'd anticipated, especially since we'd just been holding hands. It was almost as though the bright lights illuminating the gas station had changed her.

"Sure. I'll see you inside in a few minutes." I smiled warmly at her and continued. "Don't turn into an icicle. It'd be terrible to come out and find a snow monster here in your place. I don't think that I'm brave enough to drive the rest of the trip with a snow monster in my car."

Sheryl' formality evaporated. Laughing, she replied after barring her teeth and growling. "Grrrrr. You be careful or I'll use my icy fangs and bite you! Then they'll have to wait 'til spring for you to thaw out."

As I turned to go in, I surprised myself by saying over my shoulder "Sheryl, you sure are fun to be around. I'm glad I had to work late and you needed a ride home. It would've been so boring having to do this alone." Turning back towards her again I asked nervously. "Are you sure you don't need a ride back to the Y in a week or two?" *Please say yes.*

"I might. I hadn't really thought about when I was going to go back. My brother and his wife will be visiting this year and they'd talked about making a drive out to Utah to visit old friends before flying back to Washington. I'd thought that I'd just tag along with them when they went."

Well, you can't ask her to choose you over her family. I thought. Disappointed I replied "I wouldn't pass up an opportunity like that if I were you." I paused as if to emphasize my next statement. "But if, for any reason, you find you do need a ride back, I'll be going back on the 30th."

"Thanks - it's nice to know that I've got an alternative, even if it's with a boy who's afraid of the snow monsters." She winked at me and then turned to start the gas pump. I just stood there for a few seconds and willed my pulse to slow down. She'd only been kidding but it still felt like I was in deep water and sinking fast. Until now I was just angling to get a date with her and not being able to steel my nerves enough to ask. *Where's the old Bill, the one that can't talk with a female fish without blabbering.* I thought to myself as I turned back toward the store I decided that before we made it to Denver *or before the old Bill comes back.* I was going to ask her out. *Things are going good Bill. You need to ask her.*

We knew we were already running late and the store keeper had said that there'd been some problems with snow sticking to the road up near the Eisenhower Tunnel and so we quickly got back on the road. I was feeling much better now and so I was driving. In our worry over the weather report we didn't get back to our little game so I didn't get to hold Sheryl's hand anymore. Besides, we'd already said our prayer. There wasn't any other pretext I could think of to get her to hold my hand which only dampened my spirits a little. We talked for a few minutes and then she fell asleep.

The roads were good until we made it past Parachute. Then the snow started falling again and with every mile it seemed as though the night got whiter. I slowed down a little then. By the time we made it to Glenwood Springs the shoulders of the road had nearly a foot of fresh snow on them and the snow plows were getting behind. A few miles further, the road started to ice up and we had to slow down even further. *This doesn't look good. We should probably turn back.* Looking down at my odometer I realized we were closer to Vail than we were to Glenwood Springs. *No. We can make it to Vail. Besides, if we have to stop I've got water and blankets in the trunk. We'll make it ok.*

Sheryl was sleeping with her head leaned against the window and I had the oldies station playing softly on the radio when I heard the announcement.

"Travelers alert! This is a traveler's alert. Earlier this evening the Colorado Highway Patrol closed interstate 70 at Vail Pass to traffic in both the east and west bound lanes. The closure is due to icy road conditions and a multi-vehicle accident in the east bound lanes near the summit. Eastbound travelers are advised to exit the freeway in Vail and await further notification on this station so that the snow and emergency equipment can clear the road. Now back to the age-old sounds of Air Supply ... *Girl, you're every woman in the world to me ...* "

Somehow I'd been expecting this to happen, but it still frustrated me. Looking at my watch, I noticed that it was now nearly four in the morning. We were only about ten miles west of Vail and on good roads, we should've been nearly to Denver. Mumbling to myself, I slowed down yet again to let a snow plow past me so that it could clear the road better than it was now. Adding to my frustration, the snow plow just kept on moving east, not even attempting to work on the current stretch of road. I was also getting tired and sleepy so I knew that we should pull over soon if for nothing more than a cocoa break to wake me up.

Sheryl stirred next to me and rubbing her eyes, asked rather tiredly "was that the radio, or was I dreaming?"

"That depends" I smiled to myself. "Were you dreaming that you were on a beach in Hawaii?"

"No, it was Tahiti. Actually, I thought I heard something about a road closure?" She mumbled with an absentminded grin on her face.

"No, you heard right. The CHP closed the interstate about 15 miles ahead. They said something about an accident and heavy snow. They didn't say when they expected to reopen the road though."

Sheryl arched her back with her arms stretched out in front of her as she tried to loosen up the muscles that had started to cramp from sleeping. "When the Highway Patrol closes a road like that, it's usually not until morning." She said casually. Fully awake now Sheryl looked over at me and frowned. "You look tired. What time is it?"

"Nearly four."

"Wow - were the roads really that bad?" She asked incredulously. "It took us nearly three hours to get here from Grand Junction, it usually only takes about two."

"Yes. Just past Parachute I had to slow down as the storm intensified."

"You should've woke me up to keep you company. I feel bad now."
She chided.

"Don't worry about it. I was doing fine until a few minutes ago when my day seemed to catch up with me. You woke up just in time. Besides, how else was I to learn your deepest secrets?" *Lets have a little fun here.*

Sheryl's hand quickly jumped to her mouth and her eyes grew to the size of golf balls. Clearly panicked, she muttered through her hand. "I didn't! Oh please tell me that I didn't talk in my sleep! I'm so embarrassed! What did I say?!" She grabbed my arm and leaned into me to look at my eyes as I glanced over at her. Her eyes pleaded "Please Bill, what did I say? Nothing embarrassing I hope." *Oops.* I thought. *This may be a little too much fun.*

I felt bad that I was teasing her, but then it was nice to have her near me. It wasn't holding hands, but it would do. I was just joking with her of course. *How was I to know that she really did talk in her sleep?* Reaching over briefly with my left hand I patted hers still clutched to my forearm. "Nothing much, just something about some clumsy nerd of a guy that head butts you, throws you into snow drifts, and then strands you in a romantic ski village overnight. I figured you were talking about David so I pretty much ignored it."

It didn't take her long to realize that I was making fun of her and in a voice indicating her relief she replied. "Well, at least we know that it wasn't a nightmare. Honestly though - I did keep my mouth shut when I was sleeping didn't I?"

The pleading look in her eyes and the intensity of her posture indicated that she was terribly embarrassed to think that she'd been talking in her sleep and hoped that she hadn't said anything she aught not to have. I didn't feel right about continuing to tease her so, laughing, I replied. "No Sheryl, you didn't say anything." *It was my attempt at joking with you that lead me to say what I did.* "I really didn't know that it would embarrass you so much to say that. I was just joking. I'm sorry." Her body relaxed a little and as a mischievous glint sparked to life in her eyes I knew that I was going to be the victim next.

Hoping to forestall the inevitable a little while longer, I continued. "I wouldn't have listened even if you did talk in your sleep. That's unless you were dreaming of me. Then I'd have to say something to defend myself." Almost too quickly she broke eye contact and ducked her head, but not before I saw the flush rushing to her cheeks. *You'll only mess things up if you press on with this line of conversation.* I told myself. *You seem to be hitting really close to the truth.* It scared me a little. I always seemed to mess things up with girls when I realized that they might be returning some of my feelings. I was just too ham-fisted when it came to things like that. As I politely looked away and pretended to have not seen her blush, I heard children giggling.

Sheryl wasn't done with the conversation though and as she let go of my arm and leaned back into her seat she asked. "Bill, lets suppose that I was dreaming of you. Would that have bothered you?"

Stammering I tried to hide my own blush as we pulled off the freeway in Vail. "I - I'm not sure. W-Why?"

Sheryl didn't say anything.

"Sheryl?" I asked as I glanced over at her. She was intently studying her purse and fingering the clasp that opens it. I figured she would say something when she felt like it.

After another minute she hesitantly started to speak. "I'm sorry. That was too forward of me. The truth of the matter was, I wasn't dreaming as much as I was thinking about you, Jed, and Alice. Jed seems to be a great person and it certainly sounds as though Alice was the perfect Samaritan. I admire people that can make lasting friends out of complete strangers as easy as it seems to be for you."

"To hear you talk" she rushed on. "Jed and Alice could be your grandparents or something yet you rarely saw them except when you passed through to buy bait or gas. I admire that in you and envy you for your friends." With the last bit still on her lips she looked up from her lap and out the passenger's window.

This time it was my turn to not have anything to say. I wasn't sure of what I could say but I felt that I had to say something. Deciding to just trust my feelings for a moment I let my heart start talking. "I - uh - I'm not sure what to say. Thanks Sheryl but it really wasn't me as much as it was Jed and Alice. They truly are Samaritans. I'm just a simple nerd with no social talents worth mentioning. Most of the time, I stumble over my tongue or say the wrong thing and mess everything up. Take you for example: I've been looking forward to this trip for two weeks, ever since we met in the Wilkinson center." I decided to go for broke. "I wanted to get to know you better but what's the first thing I do? I head-butt you into the snow from inside your own house and then bore you stiff talking about oxidation states in chemistry. What I really wanted to do was convince you that I was more than the nerd than I appear and to see if perhaps you'd consider ever going out with me when we get back to Provo. I don't ... " I didn't get to finish because as soon as I pulled the car into the parking lot of a small doughnut shop Sheryl interrupted me with a little sniffle as she brushed something from her eye. Before I could compose myself to apologize for my forwardness, Sheryl began.

"I like you Bill. I like you the way you are, and I like the sincerity you've got and yet seem to be unaware of. A girl could grow to love you for that." She was nearly whispering. "You've got a way about you that makes everything you say and do a compliment to any girl you're with. I noticed this tonight." She looked up from her lap and engaged my eyes briefly before continuing demurely.

"I've never had a date, or even just a friend, consider me important enough or special enough to hold my car door open and then, once I'm seated to lock the door as they closed it. Yet you've done this every time we've gotten into the car. I'm just a tag along on this trip, yet with the very minor exception of the chemistry lecture" She looked up out of the corner of her eye with a wain smile on her lips before continuing. "I've thoroughly enjoyed myself and felt completely at ease and safe with you. That's why it's hard for me to say that right now - with David and all - I don't know that it would be a good idea for us to go out."

She seemed to anticipate my interrupting her so she rapidly continued. "I don't want to say that I won't go out with you, only to say that I've got some things to sort out in my head about David. I'm sorry if I've misled you until now. It certainly wasn't my intent but David and I've been talking about getting engaged. I told him I'd have to think about it over the holidays." She continued as if to herself. "It took some convincing to get me to agree. Now you step in and confuse the issue." As I started to apologize, Sheryl held up her hand to my mouth and continued. Her sniffles seemed more pronounced now and my vision seemed to get a little blurry.

"No - let me continue. In a way, I think that I'll eventually be glad for the confusion. Just tonight, I've had my eyes opened about a few things and I need time to work them out. You're a great friend Bill. I almost feel as though we've known each other for years instead of the few weeks and hours that we've spent in class or here in the car." She looked up at me through moist eyes. "I know this isn't what you'd hoped to hear but please understand. I think that in all honesty - if David and I ever do break up then I'd be happy to go out with you." There were tears in her eyes now as she looked over at me and, with a tenderness that I'd longed to feel from her, she brushed her hand along the side of my face. It came away wet. I hadn't realized that there were tears in my own eyes. For some reason I wasn't ashamed either. The tears explained why it appeared as though Sheryl was melting when I looked at her. Before she buried her face in her hands, she sniffled. "I'm sorry."

We both sat quietly in our thoughts for a long time. I'd turned the engine and the heater off as we pulled up into the parking space and now, as we took time to compose ourselves, the car got colder and colder and I imagined that it was my heart dying. I'd thought things were going in my favor and then David steps in to take it all away. I wanted to scream and yell and just vent all of my frustrations but I couldn't. I didn't know how. I wasn't even sure if I had a right to. Instead I swallowed hard and replied. "I understand." *I did it again. I imagined myself into a delusion.* I paused for a moment and then, opening the door, I continued "I'm going to see if there's anything to eat in there." Nodding toward the doughnut shop "Do you want to come in?"

"No." Was her reply. "I think I'll stay here. Thank you though."

As I closed and locked the door to the car, I remembered what my bishop had said years ago in my sixteenth birthday interview. *"Bill, the prophet has said that you can date now. The young women that you'll be escorting are daughters of your Father in Heaven. They, their fathers, and their Heavenly Father have entrusted them to your care during the hours that you are their escort. Their safety, their virtue, and their very lives depend on where you take them, how you treat them, and your skills as a driver. Their safety and security should be the most important thing on your mind. From when you escort them from their home, to your car, and then back again after your date. Open their doors for them. Never take them to places that are dangerous or unsafe for them physically and spiritually, or harmful in any other way. Remember that you're responsible for their safety while they're in your car and in your care. Be sure that you've got them safely secured in the automobile in the event of an accident. Be the best driver on the road, which means, be the safest.*" It'd never occurred to me that a simple thing like locking the car door as I closed it on a date could mean anything special, I'd simply developed that habit and forgotten about why. Sheryl was the first woman that I'd met since returning from my mission to make me realize that the attitude that I'd sought to develop when escorting my dates, what few there'd been, had become second nature to me. More importantly, now I realized that at least one woman appreciated them.

As I returned to the car having found the store to be sold out of any food, because of the road closure eight hours earlier, I tried to convince myself that Sheryl's rejection of me had some beneficial purpose. At least I'd made a good impression on her without ever knowing it. Perhaps I wasn't so clumsy socially as I'd always thought. Unlocking the door and getting in I told Sheryl what I'd discovered.

"There isn't any food for sale here. The road closure's been a big plus for the local merchants, the guy behind the counter indicated that most of the other stores in the area are also sold out of quick snacks and foods." Shrugging my shoulders, I glanced over at her "We can have all the coffee that we can drink though - free."

Sheryl laughed nervously. While I'd been gone, she'd composed herself and though there were still small pillows under her eyes she smiled warmly as I settled into the car seat. "A good thing for them that we don't drink coffee then isn't it."

"I guess it is." I laughed. "I hadn't thought about it that way before."

"I turned the heater on and was listening to the radio while you were gone. They said that the accident's been cleaned up and that the plows are out cleaning the road now. They hope to have it open, and sanded, by dawn if not earlier." Sheryl seemed apologetic. "I'm sorry that you had to wait for me to finish my final before we left. You at least wouldn't have gotten stuck."

I didn't want her thinking that this whole mess was her fault so I tried to cheerfully reply. "It's ok. Besides - If I hadn't waited then you'd have been here alone in your car. I did make an extra two dollars today in commissions that I wouldn't have had if I'd left earlier this morning. I'd offer to buy you a candy bar or something with my windfall but I'm told that, though I'm rich, I'm not rich enough to make food appear from thin air like the Savior did in the New Testament." I'd decided to lighten up the mood a little and, hopefully, forget about the earlier incident.

Sheryl straightened her shoulders and impishly smiled back at me as she began speaking in a formal tone. "I appreciate the offer kind sir but might I be permitted to share this with you thereby allowing you to save your fortune for another day." As I turned to see what she was indicating, my coat, which had gotten caught in the door as I closed it, ripped open and the down filling burst into the air and was caught up in the air currents from the heater fan.

The feather blizzard proceeded to fill the car and cover the half-melted Hershey's bar she held in her hand. We both watched in horror as the dark chocolate seemed to vacuum the feathers from the air and at the same time sprout wings. A moment later, as we laughed uncontrollably, we began to pluck our chocolate turkey so that we could carve it up and eat it for our holiday repast.

We had to turn the heater off long enough to allow the feathers to settle sufficiently for us to be able to make progress at cleaning the candy bar. By the time we finished, half of the chocolate was on our hands as if they'd sprouted wings. It must've been a thrilling site for the donut shop manager to see two bird-people feeling their way toward the bathroom to clean up. With every step, dropping clumps of feathers and chocolate to mix with the melted snow on the floor. Later, after we'd managed to blow most of the remaining feathers out onto the ground, Sheryl nervously commented. "I've got a *Snickers* bar in my purse but after what you did to the last peace offering I made to you I don't think that I should bring it out." Her voice was nearly drowned out by her efforts to not bust out laughing again.

Chuckling myself, I replied. "I agree with you. My belly's sore from laughing so hard that I would probably get sick if I were to eat any of it anyway."

"That's probably a good thing then. I'd promised my mom I'd give this one to her."

This sounded ridiculous to me. *Why in the world?* "What? Don't they have *Snickers* bars in Colorado? Can't she just go to the store and get one? Last time I went shopping they had them." Before Sheryl could answer, the radio announcer came on to say that the pass would open in three hours and that stranded travelers could continue on their way east at that time. Letting my earlier outburst pass I continued. "Well that's good news. I think, if you don't mind, that it'd be in both of our best interests if I were to take a little nap while we wait. I'm tired."

"I think that'd be a great idea." Sheryl replied. "I've had my nap so I think that I'll listen to the radio if that won't keep you awake." Sheryl replied. Then, as if it really mattered to her that she offer an explanation she continued. "By the way, they do have chocolate bars in Colorado but mom thinks that the Utah ones taste better." She rolled her eyes at me to indicate what she thought of the idea too.

"That's silly." I said sleepily. "The Utah ones and the Colorado ones probably came on the same truck from the factory. There's no logical reason that they should taste different. It's a good thing that I'm not hungry right now or I might have to do a scientific study starting with that *Snickers* bar in your purse." Sheryl laughed as I drifted quickly off into sleep.

5

I was surprised at how difficult it'd been to tell Bill that I couldn't date him when we got back to BYU. I really felt bad, but David and I'd been talking about marriage and in some way I felt that it would have been wrong to be dating someone else while contemplating marriage to another. I knew that I'd hurt Bill terribly. He'd been angry when he went in to get some doughnuts and I knew that he needed to be alone. I wasn't prepared for the complete change in attitude when he came back though. He didn't seem to be angry anymore, though his eyes still radiated the bleeding of his heart.

The shock on his face when his coat tore, filling the car with feathers, was priceless. I'd never laughed so hard in my life. After we'd gotten the feathers cleaned up Bill also seemed to be more relaxed and to have accepted my previous rejection. I didn't like to call it that, it seemed too cold, but rejection it was. David would've been poor company the rest of the trip if it'd been him, instead of Bill that I had turned down.

I was feeling a little more apprehension about getting engaged to David. I told myself that it was probably just nerves even as I questioned my motives. Was I ready to settle down? Was he the right one? Did I love him?

How could I be sure that he was right when he said *"Sheryl, you and I are supposed to be together forever - I just know it! I've got a testimony that the two of us are right for each other. Will you trust me and at least be my girl?"*

I'd told him a month ago that I would think about it and wouldn't date other guys but he needed to give me some time. I hadn't accepted any other dates since then. Recently, I'd even begun to feel that I had the right kind of feelings for him. That perhaps, he was the one.

Since then, David had started being more persistent in his wanting to be near me and cuddle up to me and sometimes it felt awkward. Whenever I got too uncomfortable, I'd push him away and get up to go get a drink or something. David never seemed to like that. He always seemed to be annoyed and a little upset that I was rejecting his advances. One time, a couple of weeks ago, he'd even made a scene.

We'd been at family-home-evening and were listening to the lesson. Cynthia and Paul were teaching it. They'd decided that we, as a family-home-evening group, needed to learn to relax more and not let school stress us out so much. With finals coming it sounded like a good idea to me. While they were teaching us meditation techniques, I was following their lead and was sitting on the floor in the lotus position. My legs were crossed in front of me and my arms were bent at the elbow with my hands resting on my knees. I'd had my eyes closed and was beginning to understand what it was that Cynthia was explaining *"...let the inner sea of your mind wash against the beaches of your eyelids. Allow it to strip away the stress and frustrations that are poisoning the unity of your spirit and body."* Then David sat down behind me.

At first I didn't know he was there because I was so intent on reaching inside myself and relaxing. When he grabbed me from behind, one leg on either side of me and pulled me backwards into his chest. It surprised me and I let out a little squeak. Cindi, my roommate from southern Utah, later told me that it sounded like a baby pig that'd just been stepped on. That of course disturbed all of the others that were trying to learn to meditate. Cindi had openly glared at us.

David wouldn't let go of me and buried his face in my neck as he pulled me up against him. *"Hey peaches, lets go outside for a little walk. This is boring and we can relax just as easily on a bench down by the botany pond as we can here. What do you say?"*

I was annoyed that he'd interrupted my concentration and besides it felt a little too good having him hold me that way and it scared me. My neck was tingling and the feel of his warm breath as he whispered into my ear made me shudder in parts of my body that I knew shouldn't be reacting. It wasn't right and I wondered if I was going to need to go talk with the bishop afterward. It was a new sensation and I didn't want it to end, but I knew that it wasn't right. Besides, I'd been tense recently and wanted to learn what Cynthia and Paul were teaching. Not trusting my voice I shook my head no and tried to sit up again.

David wouldn't let me up. *"Come on. It'd be good to get out of this hot house. Lets go cool off on the porch."* Then he kissed my neck as he started to stand up and pull me with him.

About a week before, we'd started to kiss goodnight after our dates on a pretty regular basis. He'd been eager ever since then to have more than the one or two kisses I was willing to offer. Until then, he'd been respectful of my feelings. This was the first time he'd ever kissed me without my permission, and the intimacy that it reflected and my body's response to it was more than I was prepared to deal with at that time. My body started, to stand but my mind was screaming at the feeling of wrongness that'd come over me. Turning toward David I quietly whispered as I prayed for strength to resist. *"David. I really don't want to go outside right now. I want to learn these relaxation techniques. How about waiting a few minutes? Paul's almost done. Then we can eat our desert with the others or outside if you want, but after the closing prayer."*

My words had the desired effect. David quickly let go of me and since he'd drawn me halfway to standing I fell back down with a rough little bounce. In a cool voice David looked at me sitting there on the floor at his feet and said *"Whatever your highness wants. I'll just go into the kitchen then."*

His voice had been more than a whisper. As he stalked out of the room, I looked around with a flush rising in my neck. The others were hiding their eyes pretending not to have heard anything. Cindi was the only one that seemed to not be embarrassed by witnessing the whole thing. She was clearly amused at his frustration. David had never been her favorite person. *"That guy's just too much like the gelding that we have around the farm back home. He struts and snorts like the stallions but in the end he's not worth too much. Sheryl he's not right for you! Don't you see that?"* To see him leave was always good news to her.

Later, more privately, David apologized to me as we walked back to my apartment. We didn't kiss goodnight that night. I was still a little shook up from the earlier contact with David and I didn't trust myself.

Remembering, as I sat in Bill's car listening to the radio, I shuddered. The way that my body had felt and reacted to David's breath and the kiss was the most appealing sensation I'd ever experienced and my palms started to sweat just remembering it. There wasn't any doubt that my body had feelings for David - it was my mind that was trying to decide if my heart was his too.

I found myself wondering what Bill would've done at family-home-evening. I knew that he'd have been one of the ones that were trying to meditate no matter how corny or stupid it seemed to him. *Bill would never have reacted that way.* I sighed at the comforting thought. My mind turned to other things and soon I found that my thoughts had focused again on Bill.

I wondered what it'd feel like to kiss him and to be near him. Would he be as persistent as David had been? Would he have stopped after I'd shook my head indicating that I didn't want to leave family-home-evening? Suddenly, Bill's car was too cramped and confining and the steady breathing, with an occasional bout of snoring, coming from the seat next to me was too distracting and intimate. I had to get out and clear my mind. Why was I fantasizing about Bill? Glancing at my watch, I noted the time. "I'm just too tired. I've got to clear my head."

Next to me Bill mumbled something and smacking his lips went back to his slumber. While he continued to sleep in the car I got out and called home using a pay phone in front of our parking spot. Mom had been sitting up reading while she waited for us and was glad to hear from me.

"Hi mom, I'm sorry but we're stuck in Vail. The road closed while we were driving from Grand Junction. The highway patrol says that they hope to open it between seven and eight in the morning."

"Sheryl dear! I'm so glad to hear from you. I was getting a little worried. When you called from Grand Junction I turned on the news and they were saying the storm was getting worse. I had a prayer that you'd be safe and after that I knew that you'd call. I've been having a wonderful time sitting here in the living room reading."

"You really should be asleep mom."

"So should you pum'kin. Until about an hour ago though, I was talking with your brother. He's got some very exciting news for you when you finally do get home."

"Really?" I was intrigued now "What does he want to announce this time?" My brother always made big announcements out of revealing secrets.

One time, when he was in high school, he made a pageant out of whom he was going take out on his first date after he turned 16. He'd invited the whole neighborhood and set up a stage in the back yard. Then he'd proceeded to play the dating game with himself as the bachelor and three "lucky contenders" as his guests. It helped of course that there were lots of girls who seriously wanted to date him and three of them were interested enough to go along with his production. Thomas wasn't an ugly man by any stretch of the imagination and he knew it! He ended up taking all three of the girls out for ice cream the night of his birthday. They've all been friends ever since. Holly just ended up being a better friend than the other two because, after his mission she was still there waiting for him.

"Sheryl, you know that I don't tell your brother's secrets. But since it isn't much of a secret any more I'll tell you. I'm going to be a grandma! Can you believe it?! Thomas and Holly are going to have a baby! Now don't you go letting him know that I told you. Act surprised when you find out from him."

No wonder mom couldn't sleep. With me on the road stuck in some snow storm and her all excited about graduating from being "Mom" to being someone's "Grandmama." I was glad to hear that Thomas was going to be a father. He and Holly had been married for nearly three years now, but I wasn't so sure that I was ready to be an aunt. Aunts were always the old ladies that gave kids candy and pinched their cheeks while blubbering about how cute junior's grown up to be. "That's great!" I said. "Now I've got to go get a bag of candy and horn-rimmed glasses."

Mom clearly didn't understand. "Whatever for dear? Don't you like your contacts anymore?"

"No mom. It isn't that. It's just that if I'm going to be an aunt then I've got to look and act the part."

Laughing now, mom replied. "Well, we won't flatter your Aunt Edna by letting her know that she's your ideal of what an aunt should be. Oh dear, I've missed you and your humor while you've been away at school. It'll be nice having you home for a while."

"I know mom. It's always nice to come home. Please give daddy a big hug for me and I'll see you later."

"I will pum'kin. Oh! Don't hang up just yet. I forgot completely, with Thomas' announcement and all. A young man called for you. He left his number and wanted you to give him a call when you got in."

"Who?"

"I think he said his name was David."

"Oh! He was going to call when his plane landed." *Why aren't I more excited?* "He's spending Christmas at a condo with his family in San Diego and he didn't know the telephone number there so he said that he was going to call when he got there. I'll call him when I get home."

"Is this the young man you've been seeing at BYU?"

"Yes mom and yes we'll talk about it. Right now though I need to get back to the car and warm up. It's freezing out here by the telephone. I promise to tell you all about David when I get home so save up all of your questions."

"Ok dear. I trust you. You've always made the right decisions. I look forward to hearing about David and meeting Bill. Remember to bring him in when you get here. I'll have something warm for you to eat. I'll see you when you get here. Drive safely."

Why did she have to link the two in the same sentence? I'd been enjoying the conversation until then. The rest of the conversation was a blur of conflicting thoughts as I tried to sort out the chaos that was bottling up my stomach when I thought about Bill and David in the same breath.

Mom said that she'd call Sister Wright and let her know that we were ok. I told her that we thought it'd probably be as late as lunch before we got in and that she should get some sleep and not worry. Mom, being the person that she is, probably went right back to her book and ignored my advice.

On my way back to the car I noticed that the sky was lighter. Though sunrise was still another hour or so away the clouds had lifted and the moon was high overhead. The wind was nearly gone now and so the still air was crystal clear. Looking to the south, I noticed the lights of four or five big snow cats out on the slopes preparing for the day's skiers. *The ski resorts must be happy about the snow.* I just hoped that the road wouldn't be too much more trouble for us, although I hadn't had a more pleasant trip to Colorado that I could remember. Bill seemed to just live life as it came. The rough parts as well as the beautiful ones too. I wished that I could handle adversity so well.

As I opened the car door, the last zephyr of the storm kicked up a few feathers that we'd missed in cleaning the car after Bill's coat gave its all to our cause. The abrupt change in temperature in the car woke Bill more rudely than I'd expected.

......

Suddenly it was ice cold. The wind blew a few feathers that we must have missed and one of them found my nose as I grumbled groggily. "Waa . . . aah . . . aah cheew! W-What's going on?" Then seeing Sheryl getting into the car I mumbled apologetically, "Oh! Sorry Sheryl. I don't always wake up so abruptly. You go for a walk or something? This late at night that could be dangerous?"

Indicating the telephone on the wall of the donut shop twenty feet away she replied "No. I just couldn't rest and decided to call home to tell my parents that we're ok. I told mom that if we have good roads that we'll be in before lunch. She was going to call your mom in a few minutes and let her know our plans as well."

"Thanks. I was going to call just before we got on the road again, but now I won't have to." Rubbing the sleep out of his eyes, he continued. "You seem to be close to your mom."

She looked a little surprised but asked. "What makes you think that?"

"Oh, I don't know - you talk about her a lot and when I spoke with her on the phone I could tell that she, at least, thinks a lot of you. Besides, I can't imagine anyone importing *Snickers* bars from out of state just for some common everyday parent. Speaking of which - what's the possibility of our sharing that chocolate bar. I'm famished."

Laughing Sheryl flung her hair behind her and folded her arms across her chest. "You have mom pegged that's for sure. She's certainly not your everyday run of the mill mom. She sometimes just drives me crazy with the super powers of hers. I wish at times that I had some kryptonite. As for the candy bar, can I buy you some donuts and hot chocolate instead? The donut shop just reopened with fresh donuts. Their cook arrived about an hour ago."

"Ok. I guess that a glazed donut is a little healthier than a chocolate bar from Utah. Now, if it had been one of those Colorado varieties I'd have to discuss this in greater detail with you." I noticed that Sheryl had a small drop of melted snow getting ready to drip from her chin. She must've picked up a little snow while on the phone. Reaching under my seat I extracted a Kleenex from the box stored there and blotted Sheryl's chin. Giving her a wink, I said, "You obviously must think that the donut is the better choice or you'd not be drooling. Or is it the hot chocolate?"

Catching onto the moment seemed to be Sheryl's talent. "Actually I was relishing the opportunity of eating such a fine gourmet breakfast in the presence of one such as yourself, a scientist of great stature, an honorable priesthood holder, a gentleman and laurel poet of English 310."

Confused I replied. "Thank you, I think I know where you're coming from on the priesthood thing and I'm going to be a scientist. I'm just not well known yet. The gentleman thing is still out for question, but I'm an utter failure when it comes to poetry. I don't think that I told you but my final exam in English was a bust. I had to write something creative and all I could come up with in three hours was four lines. It's a good thing that I don't have any D credit yet or I wouldn't be able to graduate. I'm grateful that I can still handle the poor grade on my transcript. I'm going to fail that one after the final."

Sheryl was smiling now. "That's not what I hear.

Listen, ever so softly to the word-heavy melody

Of love and peace.... "

In total bewilderment I interrupted. "What! Where'd you hear that?"

"Now Bill, didn't your mom ever tell you that you shouldn't interrupt a girl when she's reciting poetry to you by the light of the full moon and a neon 'Winchels' sign? It destroys the ambiance and the romantic mystery that good poetry brings into a moment such as this."

"Yes, but... No, but... Aw shucks you've got me so confused right now I don't know which way's up. Obviously you've seen my English final. I've never been so embarrassed in my life and here you are a published poet, or at least, I remember your saying that you had published some stuff. Poetry was one of the things you'd mentioned. I think I need to go hide under that tree over there."

Obviously Sheryl was enjoying herself very much. I on the other hand felt like I was on fire. I knew that my face was flushed and yet I couldn't bring myself to look away. Her eyes were alive with mirth and her face seemed to glow in the wash of light seeping through the windshield. A halo of silky brown hair billowed around her face framing it in walnut. Her lips, slightly parted, were turned up and glowing in the red neon discharge of the store's open sign. I knew at once that I was falling madly in love. The only thing that saved me was those kids, Thomas and Sophia.

Shhh!! Thomas, dad's going to kiss mom. Don't interrupt them. It's rude! It is not! Is too! Is not! Is too! Is . . . Shaking my head to clear it I heard the remnants of laughter echoing through my thoughts as one in particular seemed to glow in my mind's eye *Listen . . . Forgotten threads of divine intelligence.*

"Seriously Bill, earlier this morning, er . . . yesterday morning, I was returning a book that I'd borrowed from Professor Freeborn. She showed me one of the final exams that'd been turned in from her creative writing class. She said that it was one of the most creative and deserving final exams that she'd ever had turned in. We talked about it for nearly 30 minutes before she told me whose it was. She wants you to submit it to a writing contest when you get back. I wouldn't be surprised if you graduate without any D credits."

I didn't know what to say. I was fully awake now and I was at a total loss for words. *Tell her thanks dad! Shh! Sophie be quiet!* "Uh Sophie says I should say 'thank you'."

"Who's Sophie?"

"What?"

"You said 'Sophie says I should say 'thank you.'" I asked 'Who's Sophie?' You normally would respond 'Sophie is... ' and I then would say 'Oh, then tell Sophie your welcome' At least that is the way my mother taught me to be polite."

"I uh . . . I don't know who Sophie is. Did I really say that?"

"Yes."

"Well I must've meant something like *I'm so pleased. Thank you*, though I still don't believe you. At least I don't want to believe you. I can't deny that I wrote that poem because you've read my final exam, but I still don't think it's worth that much."

In a strong and confident voice Sheryl replied. "Bill, who's the English major here? I was touched by the poem and so was Professor Freeborn. We both reveled in its sincerity. There was a real depth of thought that went into those four lines and I admire that in you. Now that I know you better I must agree, it just seems to fit you. You're so careful about everything and don't waste any words. You get to the point and communicate it well. You should be proud of that. Most people just can't communicate their feelings like you do. They spend pages and pages trying to say something short, like 'I love you' and still come up short. This is the bane of those of us who teach English. Wasted words are worthless words."

"Wow. I guess that I've got something to think about. I still can't help but to think that it was a fluke though."

She seemed to want to say something more. This time though it was less emphatic and she fidgeted with her hands in her lap as she began. "You also have a wonderful ability to forgive. I'm sorry for what I said earlier about not dating you when we get back to BYU. I've made commitments to David and I feel that as long as he holds me to those, I need to hold myself to them as well. No matter how much I'm tempted to change that." she looked up from her lap and paused, her hands still and forgotten. Her eyes held the hint of a tear as she burrowed into my heart with their level gaze. "And it was a temptation. I want you to know that. Will you forgive me for hurting your feelings earlier?"

"Yea, I understand. Don't worry about it. I've forgotten about it already. I had a companion on my mission that taught me about commitments. I'll never forget the lesson. I understand completely. Lets be friends though. Agreed? I don't think that I'll ever forget this trip. It would be a shame to not have a friend to remember it with me."

"Agreed! Now let me seal our friendship with a donut. What do you say?"

"Sounds fine with me. Then lets go home!"

......

The interstate was much improved when we were finally allowed back on at 9:00 A.M., nearly fourteen hours after we'd left Provo. We still had at least three hours to go before it was all over too. Bill seemed refreshed after his two-hour nap and not one but three glazed donuts. His excuse was that six donuts had at least the same number of calories as a chocolate bar and if he couldn't eat the chocolate bar, he at least better get the nourishment his half would've given him. I couldn't argue. I'd eaten two chocolate eclairs myself.

With the passing of the storm during the night, the sun was bright and cheery as we headed east toward Denver. Everywhere there was evidence of its passing. Cars were sprouting from snow drifts on the side of the road. Near the summit, three wrecking trucks were preparing to return to Vail with the remains of what looked like four ice sculptures shaped roughly like automobiles though one of them looked more like an accordion than a minivan.

As tired as we were, we didn't find silence to be a problem. Bill talked about his plans to go on to graduate school and eventually get a Ph.D. I told him more of my desire to maybe serve a mission. I talked about what it was like to grow up in Colorado and pointed out some of the landmarks as we passed by them. I even remembered some of the fun stories associated with them. Things like Lookout Mountain being an old robber's roost and apocryphal stuff like that. By the time that we started down the final pass into the Denver area it was a little after 11:00 and we were famished. Eager to be home, I decided that it was time to tell Bill how to get to my house.

"You can save about a half hour by using the C-470 loop to the south. I live just off of the loop near the temple."

"Really - that's in the first ward isn't it?"

"No actually it is in one of the Highlands Ranch wards. I forget which one it is now because they split just recently."

"How long have you lived there?"

"I moved there fifteen years ago when I was seven. We moved from Arizona."

"Really! I didn't know that you lived in Arizona? Where was it?"

"Tucson, in the Rincon stake, I'd forgotten that you went to Arizona on your mission. Did you ever serve in Tucson?"

"No I went to the Tempe mission. Tucson was a different mission. We did have to go there once to the University of Arizona for a regional conference. That's all I ever saw of Tucson."

"I don't remember much. Mom tells me stories about finding snakes and scorpions in the back yard. My favorite though was the tarantula that made it into the kitchen and set up house behind the refrigerator. Dad tells that story because it still scares Mom to death to even think about it."

"Tell me - it'll pass the time and divert my mind from my stomach. That is unless the spider spent time inside the fridge."

"No - it just lived near the refrigerator. The way Dad tells it, Mom was really hungry one night and decided that she could use a bowl of ice cream. Not wanting to share it with anyone, and not wanting to wake him up, she'd just crawled out of bed and didn't turn on the light. She didn't bother with her slippers either. After she got to the kitchen she decided that the moonlight streaming through the kitchen nook was providing enough light so she didn't turn on the kitchen light." I was beginning to giggle now and it was hard to school myself to continue. Glancing over at Bill, I continued.

"Well, the ice cream was in the freezer and the freezer had a light inside that went on when you opened the door. Mom got out a bowl and the ice cream scoop before she went to the refrigerator for the ice cream. As she stepped up to the fridge she felt something under her foot as she started to set it down. She said it felt like I'd left one of my stuffed animals on the kitchen floor so she just kicked it aside and didn't think anything of it. It wasn't there when she put her foot down the next time. When she opened the freezer door though, the light came on abruptly. In the few moments it took her eyes to adjust to the increased light she felt and then saw a dark blur scurry up her leg and chest and then across her arm to her hand holding the freezer door open. After her eyes adjusted, she was looking at her hand where it met the freezer door. A huge black tarantula was sitting there calmly looking back at her." I was laughing too hard now and had to take a breath to calm down before I could continue.

"She froze in shock and then let out the most blood curdling scream you could ever imagine. Shaking her hand, she started running around the kitchen screaming that she was going to die. This did something to the tarantula. It got scared and clung on tighter. The tighter it held on the faster mom ran and the louder she screamed. Dad of course woke up at the first scream and came running into the kitchen with a baseball bat and looking sleepy but ready to hit any intruder out of the park. He says that what he saw will forever be imprinted on his mind."

"Mom was running in circles shaking her hand two or three times and screaming and then she'd stop, glance at her hand and seeing that the spider was still there she'd repeat the process. After about three iterations the spider decided it was through and jumped straight up the next time mom stopped to look at her hand. This of course scared mom and she started running again. That turned out to be a mistake. This time she ran right into the spider as it came back down on her head. Dad knew enough to drop the bat and catch mom as she passed out."

"Thomas and I were up by that time. When mom came around, we were all in the kitchen and the spider was gone. After that, Thomas and I had our turns looking for the monster that had attacked our mother. When it proved to be too elusive we had a family snack at 2:00 in the morning, mom's ice cream. Dad of course had to get it out of the fridge because mom wouldn't go near that part of the kitchen. In fact, I remember eating out a lot that week."

As I finished the story, I looked over at Bill. He had the most serious face I'd ever seen. His eyebrows were drawn down and his forehead was wrinkled in thought. He rubbed his chin a little bit and then spoke.

"Hmmm. I wonder … " He paused and then shook his head. "No, it couldn't be!"

"What?"

"Never mind. It was nothing."

"Awe come on. You wanted to say something?"

Bill turned to look at me as if considering whether or not to tell me something. Then he shrugged his shoulders and turned back to the road as he began. "Well, it probably isn't related but I had a companion once that transferred into my mission from the Tucson mission, Elder Christiansen. He was a great guy but he had a pet that he brought with him. It was a big black tarantula with brown furry legs." Bill glanced over at me to see how I was reacting. I wasn't going to give him the benefit of getting me to crack a smile. He continued, "The thing must've been six inches wide with the biggest eyes you've ever seen. It was rather cool to look at. I'd never seen a spider that big. That wasn't the creepiest thing though. It was the most disconcerting thing to see him play with it. I felt sick to my stomach nine times out of ten when I'd watch them."

"He'd let it sit on his hand and wave it up and down like this." Removing his right hand from the steering wheel, Bill started moving his arm up and down while bending his wrist. It looked like he could be painting a fence if he'd held a paint brush. As his arm went up his wrist would bend down and then bend up as his arm moved down. "The spider would just sit there and as Elder Christiansen's hand went up it would scrunch down on his hand and then on the way back down it would stretch out its legs like an accordion. The spider seemed to just love it because when Elder Christiansen would stop it would jump straight up off his hand and then land in the same place. It would do that repeatedly until Elder Christiansen started swinging his hand again. This would go on for an hour or so some times."

I wasn't going to smile but the way that Bill kind of rolled his eyes to the right to see if I was listening while trying hard to appear as though he was concentrating on the road made me just crack up and I couldn't stop. I spent a few minutes trying to catch my breath. Just as I had things under control, Bill continued and left me with tears in my eyes from laughing so hard "I was wondering if it might be the same spider or at least a relative. It would be interesting to know if you and I were somehow cousins or something because our arachnid roommates were related. What was your spider's surname? Mine was Lovesflies. Spider S Loveflies." I lost what control I'd regained previously and once again I couldn't catch my breath. I was laughing so hard that I couldn't tell Bill to get off the freeway and so we missed my interchange and had to double back. We sat in the car in front of my house for five minutes while I composed myself before mom noticed and waved us into the house from the front door.

Bill grabbed my bags with a big grin and with a wink nodded toward the door "Go ahead cousin." I almost lost it again. I'd never laughed so hard in my life and I was certainly glad that I'd gotten to know Bill. He was going to be a great friend.

Mom didn't even let Bill put down my bags before she was shaking his hand and saying. "Bill. I spoke with your mother about twenty minutes ago. She and your father had to go to the store to pick something up and she wanted me to tell you that the back door's unlocked. They'll be home about 1:30."

"Thanks - I didn't bring my key so it'll help to know that when I get home."

"Since it's lunch time and your folks aren't home, would you join us for a bite before you go? Sheryl's dad wants to meet you."

"Well since there isn't anyone at home right now to welcome me. I'd be delighted. That is if you could spare a little soap and some water for me to wash up. It's been a really long drive."

"Certainly, you both could probably use a little time to clean up. Will five minutes be enough?" Both Bill and I nodded affirmatively. "Then the bathroom's just down that hall and to the right, the first door. Sheryl, will you show him and then join us in the dining room?"

"Sure mom. Com'on cousin." I took Bill's arm and pulled him toward the hall as mom looked at me strangely. I smiled at her and then winked conspiratorially at Bill.

After showing Bill to the guest bathroom I told him I'd be right back, and then quickly ran my bags to my room and used my bathroom to wash up. I had feather marks stamped in chocolate on my blouse so I changed into some sweats. I didn't want to put on nice clean clothes until I had time for a shower.

As we went into the dining room Dad stood up from the head of the table and moved around to shake Bill's hand. "Bill, thank you for seeing my daughter home safely, she's the jewel in her mother's and my life. I greatly appreciate your doing this." Indicating Thomas and Holly who were already seated he continued. "Let me introduce you to my son and daughter-in-law, Thomas and his wife Holly."

Thomas stood and shook Bills hand. "It's nice to meet you Bill. What do you study at BYU?" Holly just waved hello.

"Chemistry."

"Wow! I barely made it through chemistry. That's why I went into business. You must be pretty smart."

I noticed how Bill was feeling uncomfortable and fidgeting so I stepped in. "For some people business or English are tough to pass. That doesn't make them any smarter than anyone else. Besides we haven't had anything to eat since the donut shop in Vail this morning, let's eat." Bill seemed to be relieved that the subject had been diverted away from him. I showed him to a chair and turned to sit in mine next to him. Bill stepped back and held my chair for me before sitting in his. Dad noticed as he moved back to his seat and I saw him nodding approval with a smile directed toward Thomas.

Mom called from the kitchen that the soup was ready and then appeared carrying a large kettle that smelled heavenly. My favorite, creamed potato and cheese soup! Setting it in front of Dad, she walked around to the other end of the table and sat down. Dad offered a blessing on the food, served it, and we started to eat. Bill obviously liked potato soup too.

A few minutes later mom asked Bill when he was going to graduate. He replied that he had a little over a semester to go because he'd changed his major after returning from his mission. That of course got mom started on missions and Bill had to explain about Tempe and Arizona. Mom being the communicative one in our family proceeded to tell Bill all about when we used to live in Arizona. Every few moments, Bill would look over at me and smile surreptitiously as he continued to listen and reminisce with her about the desert flowers in winter bloom. Seeing an opportunity, I jumped into the conversation.

Reaching over to take Bill's hand under the table in an effort to warn him about what I was about to do, I squeezed it as I began. "Bill seems to think that we might be related in some way. When he was in Arizona, his companion had a pet tarantula that lived behind their refrigerator. I told him about your experience mom and he seems to think that if the spider isn't the same one then at least they have to be related genetically to want to live in the same place."

Clasping her hands over her heart mom rolled her eyes. "Heavens! What a nightmare that was. I couldn't get it off my hand. Now it's funny but I thought I was going to die!" We all laughed and Bill gave my hand a squeeze before releasing it.

"I asked Sheryl but she didn't know. Our pet went by the name Spider S Lovesflies. Do you know the family name of your spider?" Dad burst out laughing in a huge roar.

"Bill! You're all right! I don't know who our spider was but I must agree with you. It must have been another of those nefarious Lovesflies. That family was all over the south of Arizona."

Bill seemed to be a little more relaxed for the rest of lunch. After the desert he politely excused himself and I showed him to the door.

"Bill, were you planning on going to the young adult fireside Sunday night? It's going to be at the Columbine building."

"I really hadn't thought about it. I suppose I might go. Why? Do you need a ride?"

"No I could always use one of mom or dad's cars but I'd like a ride if you don't mind."

"Not at all. What time does it start?"

"Seven."

"OK then I'll swing by and pick you up at about 6:30."

"I'll be ready!" As Bill started to open the door to leave, I took his arm for a moment. "Thanks Bill for being a good friend. I needed one and you came through. I never would've made it home if it hadn't been for your help." Then I gave him a quick hug and let him go. After I closed the door behind him, mom joined me in the entry hall.

"Bill's a very nice young man. I like him. He has a good sense of humor too - Spider S. Lovesflies - indeed." With a little snort and a laugh she continued. "I didn't want to say anything until he went home, but that other boy, David, called again. He wanted you to call him as soon as you got home."

"Thanks - did you write his number down?"

"It's on the pad by the kitchen phone. If you want some privacy, you can use the office phone. I'll keep dad and Thomas off the line for a while."

"That's ok mom. I think what I need most right now is a long bath and an hour or so of rest. David can wait."

"Sure Pum'kin. I put fresh towels and toiletries in your bathroom. Do you want me to call you in an hour so you don't oversleep and ruin the rest of the day?"

"No. I'll just set my alarm. Thanks anyway." As mom turned to leave, I said "You know - you're always right. Bill is a great guy. He's the perfect gentleman as well."

Turning back toward me mom smiled and nodded her head knowingly. "Dad was impressed when he held your chair for you at lunch. He's still talking about it."

"That's just what I mean. All the way through Utah and then when we got stuck in Vail, Bill was thoughtful and kind. Even after I told him that I wouldn't be able to date him when we returned to BYU." I paused and with a big sigh continued. " I wish I'd met him a few months earlier."

"What do you mean?" Mom's radar had tuned in on something and she wasn't going to let go of it.

"Well, I'm not quite sure yet." I suddenly decided that what I really needed more than rest was to talk with mom. I continued. "Let's go in the living room for a little while."

I loved the living room. Years ago mom and dad had commissioned a huge painting of the Salt Lake Temple. The Temple was depicted late in the day as the sun was setting. The sky was filled with vivid reds and oranges while the granite of the temple, lit from below, caused the building to take on a life of its own. The temple glowed as though it was a celestial being.

They'd framed it in a four-foot by four-foot gold-leafed picture frame. It hung on the living room wall in plain sight as we entered or left the house by the front door. They'd even spent money to have an electrician install a spotlight on it so that it always had the correct light. It was the centerpiece of what mom and dad referred to as the Celestial Room of their house. They spared no expense in decorating and furnishing this room. It was always immaculately clean. We held family-home-evening and family prayer there. When a date would pick me up - Dad, Mom, or sometimes even Thomas would escort him into that room to wait for me to come down from my room.

It'd been the centerpiece of my life for many years. I always felt at peace there. I never forgot what was important when I looked at that painting. Now, I felt as though I wanted it to witness my conversation with mom.

As we sat down on the sofa I looked over at the picture and noticed how one window, high on the eastern tower seemed to glow a little bit brighter. Mom and Dad had once told me that the window was special to them. It was their window, our family's window, because on the other side of that window our family had been sealed as a forever family. It was the window to 'their' sealing room. I sighed as I thought *Someday. Someday I'll have my own sealing room.*

I told mom about David and how we'd met. I told her about our dates and interests, how he loved to dance and was always dressed in the best designer clothes. I told her about his car. We talked about how I'd agreed to not date other guys while we discussed marriage. I told her about everything even the little boy in the mall.

She listened and didn't interrupt except for a smile here, and a small tear there. Then I told her about Bill. How he was considerate and kind. I told her about Jed and Alice. I laughed with her as I described the ritual feathering of our candy bar earlier in the morning. We talked for hours until I couldn't stay awake. Mom brought me a comforter and I slept there on the couch in the celestial room of my house. I dreamed of the Lord's house and what it'd be like to sit in His Celestial Room. I was alone with my dream. No David. No Bill. Just me.

6

I called David later that night. He wasn't in so I left a message. When we finally did get to talk, it was Saturday night and we talked for nearly an hour. He told me how he'd gone to the beach earlier and went snorkeling. He whispered that he was miserable because he couldn't be with me. I joked with him about his having sunny days and warm weather while I was freezing in snow. I told him about the trip out and being stranded in Vail. He didn't like the fact that Bill and I'd spent the whole night trapped in the car by the snow. He was jealous. I assured him that Bill was a friend and nothing more. I only wish that I could assure myself of that.

Before we hung up, he asked "What're you doing tomorrow night?"

"It's Sunday night so I was going to go to the young adult fireside. I hope to see some of my old friends that are visiting for the holidays."

"Oh!? What time's it going to be? I might want to call again tomorrow."

"Seven but I'll be going at six-thirty. I should be home by nine."

"Ok. I'll call after that then. I'll talk with you later Peaches."

"David, please don't call me that. It makes me uncomfortable."

"Why? My favorite fruit is a peach and yet having you near me makes me willing to give them up all together. That's why I call you Peaches. It reminds me of how important you are to me. I don't see why it should make you uncomfortable."

"Well it does. Sorry. I have to go now. Bye David."

"Ok, I'll see you later. I love you."

Church the next day was great. Our ward always had a great choir. Sister Smyth had been an opera star in New York City before she and her husband had retired to Littleton. With her talents and direction, every year, the ward choir sang a different selection of numbers from Handel's Messiah. Her choir's performance was so famous that the Bishop once joked that it was the only time of the year that the ward's sacrament meeting attendance reached 80 per cent of the total ward population. The other wards in our building always complained of reduced attendance on the Sunday that Sister Smyth directed the choir's holiday concert.

In the evening, Bill came by promptly at 6:30. He'd shaved and had an ironed shirt on under his grey and charcoal blazer. As I got into the car and Bill closed and locked the door behind me I noticed mom and dad watching from the living room window. Mom was smiling.

The speaker was a former FBI agent who'd been in some really scary situations where he could've been killed or hurt seriously. He told us that it was his faith in his God that had kept him safe throughout the years. He said that prayer was the most powerful weapon that he'd ever had in his arsenal. It was still his weapon of choice. Now he spends his time counseling gang members from the Denver area.

As we were leaving, I introduced Bill to Shelly. Shelly was a Junior at Colorado State University and was a great girl. I'd been her peer counselor in high school. One afternoon, when we'd run out of school problems to talk about, we'd started talking about the existence of God. Shelly had been agnostic. Her parents still were. She and I'd talked about the plan of salvation. I told her what I'd been learning in seminary and she'd try and convince me that I was wrong. After a couple of weeks though she started to listen more and argue less. Then she started to read the materials that I'd given her. It wasn't a surprise to me when she announced just before high-school graduation that God did exist and that she wanted to be baptized.

Her dad was furious at her and nearly disowned her. Her mom remained aloof but she too had been deeply disappointed. Shelly was really upset by her parent's lack of support and understanding but she knew that she should be baptized so she wasn't going to be persuaded otherwise. Elder Young, one of the missionaries that had come to my house to teach her had made her a promise. *"Shelly, As a representative of Jesus Christ, and in his name I promise you that if you'll commit to being baptized in two weeks and if you'll meet regularly with Elder Jenkins and I then at least one of your parents will attend your baptism and someday you'll be reconciled with them both."*

Shelly'd believed Elder Young and had faithfully met with him and his companion over the next two weeks. On the day of her baptism, Shelly's mom had walked into the chapel and watched as her daughter was baptized. It took three years for her dad to decide to speak to her again. She was my example of how one should live the gospel, by faith. She and Bill spent nearly a half hour talking while I spent some time with a few others that were home for the holidays.

As we were driving back to my house after the fireside Bill commented. "Shelly was telling me how much you influenced her life when you brought her the gospel. She told me how you never once compromised what you believed and knew to be true when you were her counselor. From what I hear, you'd make an excellent missionary."

For some reason I was pleased that Bill thought so. "Thanks Bill." We talked the whole way home about friends and faith. The evening had been delightful so I wasn't prepared for what was waiting for me after Bill escorted me to the door at home.

David was sitting in the living room on the couch talking with my father. "David! My heavens what're you doing here? You're supposed to be in San Diego!"

David was eying Bill suspiciously as he replied. "I decided to take in a little snow and some skiing. The snorkeling was getting boring. Besides I had something I wanted to talk to your father about."

I was getting nervous now. Bill didn't seem to be comfortable either. I didn't know what David would want to talk to dad about but it could only involve me and that was scaring me. I started to shake and grow faint. Before I started to pass out, Bill grabbed my elbow and escorted me into the living room to help me to sit down. David just sat there and watched Bill as he retreated to the back of the room and frowned. Obviously Bill didn't want to be here but he couldn't think of a way to extricate himself quickly. I wasn't sure that I wanted him there either. The last thing I wanted was to hurt him again.

Mom asked "Are you ok Sheryl?"

"Yes mom. I was just surprised and got a little light headed there." Then turning to dad, I continued "what seems to be so important that David had to come all the way from San Diego?"

Glancing at Bill sheepishly and then indicating David, dad answered.

"Sheryl, David came here from San Diego to see me and to see if I was willing to let him marry you. He tells me that you've been talking about getting engaged. Is this right?" David's smile turned into a smirk as he looked toward the gasp that came from the general direction of Bill. I couldn't bring myself to look behind me at Bill. My worst nightmare had come true.

"I … I don't know what to say. David's telling the truth. We did talk about the *possibility* of getting engaged. I told mom that Friday afternoon. But I was *supposed* to have the holidays to think about it." This last was directed at David with a sharp look punctuating my point.

David took that as his cue to make a speech. Rising from where he sat next to dad, he walked over to my chair and kneeling to the side he took my hand in his. "Sheryl, I know that we said that you'd have the holidays to think about it. It's my fault that I'm here and have sprung this on you. Please forgive me. When I called Friday night and you hadn't arrived yet I thought the worst. My heart jumped into my throat and I couldn't breathe. My every thought and breath were for you, wondering if I'd ever see you again." I was getting sick to my stomach at what was happening. His tone of voice was so cloyingly sweet that it nearly choked me. "I kept wondering if you were hurt, lost, or dying in a car wreck somewhere. I panicked. I had to see that you were ok." Looking away from my eyes for just a moment toward Bill, he quickly continued. "I had to see that you were safe."

"When I couldn't sleep with worry I called the airport and made arrangements for a flight out as soon as I could make it. I'm sorry. If you'd still like to think about it please do. Would you at least wear this while you think?" Somehow he'd produced from his pocket a huge blue velvet box. As he opened the lid, I heard mom gasp and saw her hand go to her mouth. In the box was the largest diamond I'd ever seen. Surrounding the diamond was a bed of rubies and emeralds. It looked as though I could buy a house with it. "This ring's a family heirloom. It belonged to my grandmother and when her son got married he passed it onto his wife, my mom, and now I want to pass it onto the one person that means more than anything in the world to me, you. Will you take it?"

I was stunned. I couldn't move. All I could see was the ring as it started to swim in a red and green ocean. Then I couldn't see anything at all. I was crying and I couldn't stop. My mind reacted instantly except somehow my voice had disappeared. *I didn't want this. I'm not ready.* I'd wanted time to think about it and now, in front of Mom, Dad, my brother and sister-in-law, and worst of all Bill, I felt like I was trapped. I tried to tell David that I couldn't take it but Thomas was faster than me.

"Wow sis! Look at that thing. You can't say no to that! David - congratulations." Thomas was pumping David's arm up and down and Dad was joining him in offering David a heartwarming welcome to the family. I could only cry harder. Mom later told me that Bill had left during the men's celebration. He seemed to be ill. I cried most of the night without sleeping.

David was given the guest room and so he was there the next morning when I came downstairs. I still hadn't put the ring on. It was on my dresser upstairs. I was confused. I didn't want it but it was the most beautiful and 'rich-looking' ring I'd ever seen. Thomas was right - I couldn't turn a ring like that down.

David noticed that I didn't have the ring on and frowned a little before coming over and kissing me good morning. I wanted to scream. *Get away! How dare you just come up and kiss me in front of my family without even asking! As if you owned me or something. How dare you force me to wear your ring. How could you hurt me like this if you really did love me! How dare you hurt Bill that way. Bill.... Oh Bill! I'm sorry! I don't have a choice anymore. Please understand.* Instead I started crying again and ran out of the room.

Later, when I came back downstairs I was wearing the ring. David noticed and seemed to stand taller with pride. I was grateful that he didn't say anything though. I wasn't sure that I was really going to say yes. I was wearing it only to save him some embarrassment.

The next week went by in a blur. I only remember two Christmas presents. David gave me a hand knit turtle neck sweater that matched his. Bill sent over a giant sized Hershey's chocolate bar on a small down filled pillow. His note said *"Listen ever so softly... Friends, Bill"*

David didn't understand. "That's weird. Who gives a girl a chocolate bar on a pillow for Christmas? Bill sure is a weird one." I had to leave the room again and cry.

David had purchased two tickets to Salt Lake from Denver so five days after Christmas we flew back to Utah where David had left his car at the airport. After the shuttle dropped us off at the car, David fingered the alarm remote and the lights flashed and the horn beeped. Putting my bags in the trunk, David moved around to the driver's side and got in. I had to open my own door and then I was the one to lock the doors as we drove out of the lot.

The drive to Provo was quiet. David seemed to be on edge. Every time he'd said something recently I'd start to cry. I was glad that he'd learned to listen to my silence and now understood that I needed time to myself. I was still wearing his ring and so he was happy but I hadn't made up my mind if I would or ever could continue to wear it.

After dropping me off at my apartment David said that he'd call later and I went inside carrying my bags from the parking lot. Cindi was the only one home when I opened the door. He never called.

"Hi Sheryl, did you have a nice Christmas? I had a great time. Dad made the yule ham this year. It was the best that I have ever tasted. I brought some back with me. I was just about to warm it up. Want some?"

"Hi. No, I don't think so. I'm really tired and I need to lie down. If anyone calls, tell them that I'm asleep. Ok?"

"Sure thing, here, let me help you with those." Indicating my bags. Reaching across to the bag in my left hand she took it, but not, unfortunately, before noticing the ring on my finger. Her eyes grew big and her head shot up. Looking me in the eyes, she recognized that I didn't want to talk about it right now and so all she said was "It looks like you got a big Christmas present. We can talk later."

"Thanks Cin. I really appreciate it. Don't tell the others will you?"

"Sure. It'll be our secret until you're ready to tell someone."

I nodded and went through the hall to my room. I had my own room and bathroom so I didn't have to deal with Heather and Connie an hour later when they got home. I just went to bed. The ring was in my sock drawer. I'd had nightmares for the last week whenever I slept with it on.

Sometime that evening the phone rang. Heather answered it but I heard Cindi tell her that I was sleeping.

......

All I could think of as I drove through Vail on my way back to Provo was the terror on Sheryl's face that night after the fireside. Even as her father and brother were congratulating David she looked like a trapped animal that knew that it was being hunted and couldn't get away. I was surprised at how calm I'd felt as I quietly dismissed myself. Sheryl's mom saw me leave and nodded in my direction with eyes that seemed to say "I understand your feelings and I wish it were him leaving instead of you." I felt relieved to know that at least I had one supporter cheering for me.

I'd learned a lot about David in those few short minutes. He was manipulative and cunning. He knew how to get what he wanted and he didn't care how he got it or who he had to hurt to get it. He also didn't cherish Sheryl and her feelings the way I thought a future husband should.

His insincerity had been transparent to me. I was a rival in his eyes and even as he was proposing to Sheryl in his guaranteed way he'd been sizing me up, looking for the possibility of trouble coming from me. I wasn't going to let him have the satisfaction. I decided then that I was going to let Sheryl know that she had an option.

I'd begun to wonder what I could give Sheryl for Christmas even as we'd arrived at her house that first day. After David's big presentation I knew what I would give her. I also knew that she'd understand the meaning behind the gift. I was her friend and always would be. She could count on and call me at any time.

I knew that Sheryl'd flown back to Utah earlier in the day and so when I stopped for gas in Price I called her apartment. Her roommate said she was asleep. I left a message and told her that I'd call again later. It was two days later that I finally was able to reach her.

"Hi, Sheryl - this is Bill, I just wanted to see if you'd made it back ok."

"Thanks for calling Bill. Cindi said that someone had called the other night. I know that it wasn't David even though he was supposed to call. I'd hoped that it had been you."

"Yea. I was calling from Price."

"Really? How's Jed?"

"He's doing fine. His grandson was with him, a cute little six-year-old."

"That's nice."

"I just wanted to see if you're doing ok."

There was a long pause on the other end of the phone and then she began to speak haltingly "It ... It's been a rough couple of weeks. I'm sorry that you had to witness that whole mess back in Denver. I still don't believe that it happened. I'm kind of sorry it did after such a beautiful evening."

My heart ached to hear her talk about it but I'd decided to let her know that there were options and I was going to do just that. "I know Sheryl. Don't worry about me. I'm always here though if you need to talk or just need a laugh. It's you I'm worried about. Are you happy?"

"I think so. David can be hard to understand sometimes. He and I have had a chance to talk things over and we've decided that we'll tell others that we're engaged but I won't commit to a wedding date yet. I feel that I need to have that much flexibility until I decide for sure."

I cringed when I heard her say that because I knew that David felt it was a done deal and would pressure her soon enough to set a date. "Well then, congratulations. Let me know when you do set a date." It sounded so antiseptic. Perhaps it was. I felt detached from my heart as I'd said it.

"Thanks. I'll do that. Listen. I need to go. David's due to come by in a few minutes and I still have to finish my homework."

"Homework? Sheryl it's only the second day of classes!"

"I know but those crazy chemists over in the Benson building seem to think that the first day isn't too soon for a homework assignment."

"I know - I've got some already too. Well if you need any help you know who to call."

"Thanks Bill. It was nice talking with you. You're a great friend - I knew that when I opened your Christmas present. I'm sorry that I didn't get you anything."

"Don't worry about it. Have a happy life. I'll see you around." With that I hung up. At least she'd understood the meaning behind my present. I wasn't going to be forgotten quickly. Why then did I feel so lousy.

The next few days seemed to fly by. I'd looked in on Sheryl's class and found that David was also enrolled so I purposely avoided that part of the building when I knew that they'd be around. I didn't want to run into them together. The days grew into weeks and then February had come. I'd seen Sheryl around campus several times, always with David. She seemed to be happy because she was smiling and laughing.

Once I ran into her in the bookstore. She was wearing David's mother's ring. I didn't want to think of it as her ring. It looked awkward on her hand. She also spent a lot of time with her other hand crossed over it as if she was hiding it. We said hi and then she'd had to go to class.

I tried to forget her but every time I'd see her on campus with David I'd get a headache and my hand would reach for my head where we'd bumped that first night before our trip. My ears would start ringing with children's voices and I'd have to take a few aspirin.

I knew I had to do something when I started hearing voices at the bookstore checkout line as I noticed the candy display. There were chocolate bars there. Utah chocolate bars!

Before I knew it I'd bought four of them and was headed back to my office with the intent of seeing if they tasted any different from the ones that I remembered from Colorado. As I opened the first bar the children's voices grew louder and there was laughter for the first time since the trip to Colorado. With every bite I tried to determine what it was about Utah candy bars, that made them so special to cause Sheryl to import them to her mom in Colorado. With every swallow the voices would get clearer, a boy and a girl. With every laugh I saw Sheryl's face grow clearer in my mind. I didn't stop until all of the candy bars were gone.

Since the chocolate incident I'd been burrowing into my research and school work trying to occupy my mind and forget Sheryl. I spent hours reading and studying my chemistry books trying to drive those voices out of my head. I nearly went blind by looking over the latest data from my experiments as I tried to forget Sheryl's face. The sudden dull wariness that came into her eyes as I dropped her at her home after the fireside to find David in her living room seemed to haunt me.

For a while it worked. I found that school was enough to occupy my mind. As my grades improved and my understanding of the material increased I found myself running out of material to study. I then attacked my work at the store. I told myself that each customer wanted and deserved the best service and the best equipment that they could afford. I was going to make sure that they got it. My sales commissions doubled and then tripled until David came into the store one day.

David didn't recognize me and it was my turn to take the walk in customers for that day. He was looking for a new stereo system. Money was no object. It was going to be a gift for his fiancé. I turned him over to my manager when I suddenly got sick to my stomach and I had to leave the showroom floor.

It was Wednesday evening a week after David had come into my store and I was at home working on a P-chem problem when the phone rang. I wasn't in the mood to talk to anyone and since I rarely received any phone calls I didn't get up to answer it. Besides, when I did get a call it was usually my mom or my home teaching companion Mike. Mom wasn't going to call until Friday and our home teaching was done for February. It was a surprise when Kevin, my roommate, knocked on my door to tell me that the phone was for me.

As I took the cordless phone from him he gave me the thumbs up sign which was our code that there was a girl on the other end of the line. I couldn't imagine who it could be and Teri was the last person that I'd expected.

"Hi Bill, this is Teri. Have you done your P-chem homework yet?" Teri was a fellow chemist and we were in the same physical chemistry class. She was from New Mexico and sat next to me during lectures. We joked with each other a lot about being in competition for the best grade. After every exam we seemed to trade places as the head of the class. One time I'd have the higher score on the exam and the next time she would. At present she was winning but we had another exam in two more weeks. This time it was on quantum mechanics and I'd begun to understand and grasp the concepts nearly a week ahead of her so I was confident that I was well on the way to winning our next round.

She was short, about five foot two, with light brown hair. She might've been thought by some to be slightly overweight but anyone that knew her soon learned that she was very athletic and simply didn't inherit the petit bone structure of her mother. We'd been in several classes together in the two years since I'd returned from my mission. This was the first time outside of class and study hall that we'd spoken.

"I was just working on it. I'm having trouble with problem five. I can't seem to get the right form for the integration of the Hamiltonian."

"Me too! Now I don't feel so bad. I'm also stumped on number three where we've got to normalize the radial function. That's why I was calling - I thought that if anyone could help me to grasp this stuff it'd be you."

"I don't know how much help I can be. I was about to throw my books through the window when you called. I've never seen an integral like this."

"That makes two of us. Listen… " There was a pause before she continued. " …I was just about to take a break from the books too. Sometimes I just go for a jog around campus to clear my head. I usually find that a half hour or so away from homework really helps me to focus on things. I don't suppose that you run and would like to join me?"

I considered the implications of answering. Was she just being friendly and wanting to pool our resources on the chemistry problem or was she hinting at something else? I'd been trying hard to drown my feelings for Sheryl in school and at work, neither seemed to be significantly helping. I'd not been out with a girl to do anything in nearly six weeks. I was starting to find myself dreaming about Eigen values and angular momentum instead of the stuff most normal and healthy people dream about. Perhaps if I went and did stuff with a woman besides Sheryl, I'd be able to forget her. I decided that I needed a break no matter what Teri's motives were. It must've taken too long for me to say something though because she started speaking just as I opened my mouth to accept. "I…"

"Bill. I'm sorry for calling. I shouldn't have asked. In all honesty… "

"No" I laughed. "I was only trying to remember if I had any clean jogging pants before I accepted. What'd you have in mind?"

"Really?" The tone of her voice was one of utter relief and astonishment. She obviously hadn't really expected me to agree.

"Yea! It sounds fun. Besides I've been overly negligent in taking care of myself in the last few weeks. I need to get back on track. Can I meet you somewhere?"

"Sure. Lets see… You live over on Eighth North by Brick Oven don't you?"

"Guilty as charged and where's your place."

"I'm over near the old BY Academy site, about two blocks away from you, how about if I meet you at the base of the steps leading up to the Maesar building in about fifteen minutes?"

"I can do that. See you in fifteen then." After I hung up the phone, I looked outside. My window faced the east. That's why I'd chosen this room. I loved to get up early in the morning and I always felt better when the sun was there to greet me and warm the carpet at my feet. Today however, a light dust of snow was falling and I shivered a little as I started to look for my running shoes.

It was twenty minutes before I was done getting ready and made it to the meeting place. Teri was already there and was stretching out her legs. She wore a grey BYU sweat shirt and BYU blue sweat pants. Her running shoes were tied with pink laces and the ends were coiled in some kind of a spring shape. She had one leg up on the lower rail of the handrail for the steps and was leaning forward touching her toes with her head. As I casually jogged up in my grey sweats with a grass stain on the right knee she switched and began to stretch her other leg.

"Hi. Sorry I was late. I had to find my other shoe. That should tell you how bad I've been recently about running." As I spoke, the crisp evening air crystalized my breath and small puffs of smoky clouds formed around my head.

"No problem I was a little late myself. Did you want to stretch out at all before we start?

"Sure." I started to loosen up a little by wind milling my arms as I twisted at the waist. I wasn't too ambitious about it though. It just felt good to be out of the house. "What kind of a run did you have in mind?"

"Well, I normally start here, when I'm rested, by running the stairs and then taking the upper campus loop around by the alumni center to the Marriot center, up toward the MTC and Y-mount terrace, and then down 9th east before cutting back through Helaman halls to campus drive. From there, I sometimes cut through campus at the physical plant until I get to the Benson Chemistry building where I finish up by coming back down the pedestrian ramp here. It usually takes me about a half hour or so."

"That sounds fine with me." I lied. It sounded crazy to me. I usually only ran about half that distance. I didn't want to admit that though, so I told myself that I could do it without too much trouble. It was only an extra mile. I wasn't that out of shape.

I wished that I'd done more stretching exercises when we reached the Marriot Center. By the time we got to Y-mount terrace I realized I was in more trouble than I'd thought I'd be. When we finally reached the Chemistry building nearly forty minutes later, I was about to collapse. Teri'd been slowing her pace since Helaman halls to allow me to keep up. I was embarrassed when she stopped running and started walking down the pedestrian ramp with me staggering along behind her.

After a few minutes, we were nearly half way down, I'd caught my breath enough to talk. "You - <gasp> are certainly more dedicated than I ever was. I wasn't sure that I'd be able to make it this far."

"You did great!" I was disgusted that she didn't even seem to have broken a sweat. Her hair was still tied up in a pony tail with a puffy pink elastic thing. She looked just like she did before we started out. I couldn't even see any evidence that she'd just run nearly two and a half miles.

"Thanks. I don't know if my body'll think so in the morning. My calf is starting to cramp up already." My legs felt like noodles and to hide that fact I casually leaned against the handrail dividing the ramp into a pedestrian and a bicycle path. Teri was stretching out a little more, to cool down.

"Here, stretch it out like this before it cramps up too much or you'll have a real problem." She leaned into a sign post with one leg forward and bent the other stretched out behind her. Her back foot was flat on the ground.

I copied her and my leg seemed to loosen up a little. "Thanks."

"No problem. Do you really want to get back into running?"

"I probably should. I've just been spending too much time at the lab. I've got a collaboration with Dr. Sung at Stanford, we've been working on a manuscript recently. That coupled with the P-chem homework hasn't left me much time for anything else but work" That was the excuse I'd been giving my roommates when they'd tried to set me up with friends of theirs. The real reason was Sheryl. For a moment I looked at Teri and began to compare her with Sheryl. *Their eyes are the same color, brown, but the similarity seems to end there. Teri seems bulkier and less sculpted than Sheryl. She carries herself in the same sure-of-oneself manner as Sheryl but Teri seems to pound the ground as she moves while Sheryl floats and glides along.*

"That's great! Dr. Sung's a spectroscopist isn't he?" When I didn't answer Teri walked over and gave me a little friendly shove on the shoulder. "Hey! Are you zoning on me? You must be more wiped out than you look."

"What!? Oh! No I'm fine." I lied. I was red in the face as I tried to close my mind to the other comparisons that were marching through my head. Luckily the run and the cold had left me flushed in the cheeks and Teri didn't notice. I dredged up her last question about Dr. Sung and tried to sound natural when I continued. "Yea - he does X-ray absorption spectroscopy on the linear accelerator there."

"Wow - what're you studying?"

"We've got this theory about the oxidation states of… " As we talked about my research we'd begun to walk around so that our legs wouldn't stiffen up. Teri seemed really interested in what it was that I was doing and even asked a few questions that gave me some new insight into the interpretation of my data. Ten minutes later we were outside of her apartment and I had to look around to get my bearings. I'd been so involved in our conversation that I couldn't remember how we'd even gotten there.

"Bill, no wonder you caught onto quantum mechanics so fast. You're doing research that requires it. Would you like to come in for a drink of orange juice or something?"

"Sure. Since we're here, I guess it wouldn't hurt. Maybe we can look at that problem again. Your run just may've broken a few things loose in my mind that I hadn't tried."

"Wow! Lets get on it then."

While Teri rummaged around in the kitchen getting our orange juice, I sat at the kitchen table looking over her solutions for the homework. I picked up a pencil and turned her pad to a blank page and started from scratch setting up problem five. By the time that she handed me a plate of cookies to go with my juice I'd done all of the preliminary work and was ready to start reducing the terms into a form that could be easily integrated. Teri stood behind me and, with her hand on my shoulder, followed along with me. After a few moments I paused and looked at the result.

"Bill, I think you did it. Look if you take *Psi* here and combine it with the *theta* and *rho* terms you get the left side of the Taylor equality."

Looking at the terms she was pointing out, I suddenly realized that we had the answer. "Your right! You did it! If we substitute in the right side of the Taylor equality for these terms then it combines with these ones and we can integrate to get the answer. How'd you recognize that?"

Sitting down at the chair next to me she pointed to the text book sitting open in the middle of the table. There on page 420 was an example using the Taylor equality. "Wow! I was stumped until you pointed that out, even though I must've looked at that example four times at home. I must've spent nearly an hour on this." In my excitement I turned toward her and grinned. "We make a good team. How long does it take you to do your P-chem every week?"

"I don't know - I just do it and hate every minute of it. I know that it takes too much time as it is. You saved me another hour or two."

"I think we saved each other the time. Speaking of which" I looked at my watch. "I think I'd better be going home." As I started to get up, I had an idea. "Teri - You know they say two heads are better than one and I really do need to get back into shape. You proved that to me today. What would you say to trying this again next week, the run and then the homework thing that is?"

Turning toward me, she appeared to think about it a little and then sticking out her hand she said "Done! Though I confess that I'd hoped you'd like to do something like that. A few of us in the class have started meeting informally here on Wednesday nights. There are about four of us right now but we're all so lost recently that we confuse each other all the time. This homework set pushed me over the edge. I couldn't think of anyone that would be better to perhaps lead the group in this section than you. Are you interested?" She looked at me kind of sheepishly and continued. "I admit that I kind of set you up. But, in my own defense, you did say that you didn't have any plans for this evening when I called."

I wasn't sure what to say. I felt like I'd been trapped but when she offered to throw in dinner as penance I laughed and decided that I could use the break from solitary study. Besides, Teri said that dinner was going to be pizza. I never pass up pizza. About fifteen minutes later three others from our class showed up with two pizza boxes and their P-chem books.

A couple of hours later we all had decided that this was definitely a good thing to do. It seemed that there was always at least one of us that knew how to work a problem and I learned a lot teaching the others how I'd solved problem three. We decided that we'd definitely continue getting together. I was the last one to leave but as I walked through the door I turned to Teri. "So when are we going running again. You've motivated me and I need to make a commitment before tomorrow when my aching body will override any desire to go again?"

She pursed her lips thoughtfully before answering "Well I run three times a week, Monday, Wednesday, and Friday. If you wanted to go along then we can try it again on Friday if you feel up to it."

Inwardly I cringed. I was going to be sore on Friday and that was going to make the run tough, at least at first. I probably would embarrass myself and not even be able to finish. Sucking in my pride I replied. "I guess I set myself up this time didn't I? I'll try it - no pain no gain right?"

"Right - see you then."

Over the next four weeks I slowly got back into shape by running with Teri. We found that after the first week, I was able to carry on a conversation as we worked our way around campus. We started to spend more time outside of class together too, lunch here, a fireside there. I was comfortable being around her and she seemed to be comfortable with me. More important, I was not so fixated on Sheryl. Though, she still haunted me occasionally. I felt bad though. I didn't have any feeling for Teri. A few days later I found out about Todd and decided that I didn't have to feel guilty at using Teri to get over Sheryl. Todd is her missionary.

Teri was waiting for Todd to return and so she spent a lot of time working on school and keeping herself in shape. She was a little nervous about his return in August. She wasn't sure that she was ready to be a wife but each day that she got a letter from Todd she'd brighten and become more convinced that she'd been right to wait. She told me that there'd been opportunities for her to date other guys and even a proposal several months back but with each guy she'd felt only friendship. Nothing like what she felt for Todd. She was happy and I guessed that Todd just might be happy too when he got home.

One day, over lunch, I told Teri about Sheryl. I told her about the trip to Colorado and how I just couldn't seem to forget her. Teri seemed to understand and, over the next couple of weeks, tried to set me up with one of her roommates and another friend. In both cases I found that I was less than enthusiastic about dating them again. I was slowly pining away my heart. Teri stuck by my side through the whole thing and encouraged me to move on with my life yet somehow did so without preaching. I guess it was meant to be then that Teri was with me that afternoon in late March when I ran into Sheryl again.

Teri and I were in an animated conversation over the wording in the newest P-chem problem set and I was emphasizing my point rather forcefully as we turned the corner heading back to my office. Sheryl was coming the other way and I didn't see her. By the time that I knew what'd happened both Sheryl and Teri were sanding over me and I was laying on the floor at their feet. My head ached terribly and I was having trouble focusing my eyes. Sheryl stooped down and put her hand on my head above my right eye. Her eyes were filled with concern. "Bill, you're going to have a bump here. Are you OK? You really hit your head when you ran into me. It was my shoulder that knocked you against the wall. I almost fell myself."

I didn't know what to say. Teri helped me out. "Hey Bill, you're made of tougher stuff than that. Remember when you slipped on the ice two weeks ago? Come on get up and walk it off." She leaned over and helped Sheryl to lift me up off the floor. As I stood, my vision went dark for a moment and then seemed to clear rapidly. Too rapidly, I think, because I noticed that Sheryl's hand didn't have a ring on it anymore and my eyes jerked toward her face. She simply looked concerned and didn't seem to notice that I was staring at her. I had to say something and in my addled state all I could think of was to introduce Teri and Sheryl. The two had been eyeing each other warily.

"Ah. I think I'll be ok. Thanks Sheryl." Turning toward Teri I continued while attempting to convey the significance of this chance meeting with my eyes. "Teri, *this* is Sheryl. She and I are from the same town out in Colorado." Teri's eyes widened and she looked over at Sheryl with a new understanding as I continued the introductions. "Sheryl, this is Teri, my friend, my lab partner and study group leader."

As the two girls continued the introduction among themselves, I moved toward a bench a few feet away and sat down. My mind was crystal clear as I stared at Sheryl's hand. *Could I be so lucky? Has something happened? Why wasn't she wearing her ring?* I didn't even fight the vision that appeared before me.

I was sitting on a sofa in the foyer of a chapel somewhere. Two little infants were sleeping in car seats at my feet. Sheryl was across the way talking with the relief society president about Tuesday's home making meeting. Sheryl was going to be teaching a few dance steps to the sisters. I smiled to myself as I watched her finish up her conversation and move toward me so that we could go home.

It was only eight weeks ago that she'd given birth to Thomas and Sophie. Twins! To look at her now one wouldn't believe that she'd gained nearly fourty-five pounds during the pregnancy. She looked trim and fit as she'd always been but, at the same time, somehow she looked more matronly - more lovely to me. I still couldn't get over the fact that she was my wife. Standing as she came closer, I gave her a quick kiss as we turned to go home for lunch.

As I locked the car door behind her and moved around the front of the car to get in myself I heard Sheryl cooing to one of the babies that'd woken up as they were being strapped snugly in their car seats behind us. She turned to look at me as I sat down and started the car. "Bill…."

"… Bill." I nearly jumped up off the bench when I realized that Sheryl and Teri'd joined me there. I shouldn't have because I suddenly got very dizzy. Steeling myself against the nausea that engulfed my stomach, I looked up at Sheryl as she, with a slight flicker of concern in her voice, spoke again. "Are you sure you're ok Bill? Do I need to help you to the health center?" All I could do was stare at her face.

"Where's your ring?" It was the first thing that came to my mind once I regained my balance and looked down at her hand. I didn't realize that I'd spoken aloud until I looked back up.

It obviously wasn't what Sheryl'd been expecting and her right hand quickly jerked to touch her naked ring finger on her left hand. Slowly she sat down as she started shaking and her knees began to weaken. Tears were forming in her eyes. Teri, her face accusing me of some terrible crime, moved to Sheryl's side and put an arm around her shoulders.

"Look. I'm sorry Sheryl. I'm not thinking clearly right now. It seems we always meet this way." Pressing my hands to my head as if to squeeze the pain out of it I continued, "I always end up with a headache too. Today it seems, I scrambled more than just my equilibrium. I'm sorry." I didn't trust myself to say anything else. Sheryl just nodded and after a few minutes she wiped her tears from her eyes and spoke.

She didn't use David's name. Instead she almost hissed. "I gave it back to HIM." Her eyes were cold and their normal sparkle had dulled to a calculating grey. I instantly felt a mood about her that I'd never felt anywhere with anyone. She hated him and the emotions that she felt seemed to seep into the air surrounding her. Then, as if she realized that I'd noticed, her shoulders slumped and she nearly whispered "We broke up."

Nine words changed my life. Nine words did more than twenty aspirin in freeing me from my headache. *She broke up with him. She gave it back!* Sitting next to her I reached over and took Sheryl's hands in mine. She tensed up and started to back away before she seemed to realize what she was doing. I let go of her hands and gave her a little more space before saying "I honestly can't say that I'm sorry to hear that. Sheryl I *am* terribly sorry though that I hurt you with my question. If I'd of known… " For some reason my voice choked up and I couldn't say anything else. I sat there feeling terrible and wanting to cry but not knowing why. It was several minutes before I could look up from my lap. Sheryl was staring at the wall in front of her. Her back was stiff and she shook as though she was cold. Teri saved me.

"Sheryl, are you ok?" At the sound of her voice, Sheryl seemed to realize that she'd been nearly catatonic and she looked briefly at Teri before slowing shaking her head no. Then she looked over at me and, bursting into tears, buried her head on my shoulder.

Teri caught my eye briefly as she gave me the thumbs up sign (She'd been at my apartment when I'd answered the phone for one of my roommates) and waved goodbye before walking away. I nodded and then turned back to Sheryl. I somehow felt as though all she wanted was to be held. I took her head in my arms and rocked her back and fourth as she cried and cried. My heart filled with compassion for her and for whatever had caused her to feel the way that she did. Somehow I knew that she didn't want me to say anything else. After a few minutes she stopped crying but I continued to hold her and brush her hair with my hand.

8

Cindi kept our secret for nearly a week after I got back from Christmas break. I'd talked with David by that time and we'd agreed that I wouldn't set a wedding date and that he wouldn't pressure me to do so. In return I agreed with him that we'd tell others of our engagement.

I loved David but I wasn't sure that it was the kind of love that I needed to have if I was going to marry someone so I couldn't bring myself to agree on a date. I kept asking myself if I had the same kind of love for him that my mom had for my dad. Talking with mom about this, she told me that the love that I saw between her and Dad was thirty years in the making. When they fell in love and got married they hadn't felt as though it was possible to love each other more. Somehow, over the next three decades, they found that what they had felt then was only a fraction of what they felt for each other now. This only confused me more because I was certain that I had more love in me than I felt toward David.

I never woke up with an overwhelming need to see his face. I never found myself counting the minutes until we could be together again. Somehow I felt tired and relieved when he'd go home as if being with him was a battle.

My roommates were the first to notice a change in me and Cindi was there to tell me the morning of my birthday in early February.

"Sheryl. What's wrong with you? You aren't sleeping at night and you've started eating everything there is in the kitchen. I swear that you're upset about something. Com'on it's me, Cin."

"I'm fine. Really I am. I'm just a little nervous about the wedding and all."

"What wedding - you haven't even decided when it'll be. *When* you do *then* you can start getting uptight. What's really bugging you?"

"Nothing OK! Just leave me alone. I don't need your mothering you know. I have one of my own. I went to school just to get away from all this meddling. Just forget it!" I was angry. I knew that I shouldn't be but I couldn't help myself. I also knew that she was right and I couldn't bring myself to admit it.

Cindi was obviously hurt. Crossing her arms over her chest she looked at me for a few moments and then turned and mumbled as she walked out the room. "He gives you the annual production of South Africa on a ring and suddenly you're too good to talk with the rest of us. Fine! Just *be* that way. You *have* changed Sheryl, and not for the better!"

I couldn't bring myself to go after her and tell her that I was sorry, that I really did need to talk with someone. I felt caged, confined, and confused. I knew that Cindi didn't like David and would side with my doubts that he was the right one. I needed someone that would be impartial and objective. I thought about going to the Bishop and seeking his counsel but I'd missed my meetings for a few weeks because I'd attended church with David. He only went to sacrament meeting. David felt that the other meetings were too boring. *"The Sunday school teacher teaches like a green Elder and the Elder's quorum teacher barely knows his scriptures."* David said that he got more out of going for a walk or ride in the mountains on Sunday afternoon where he could feel closer to God than he did by attending his Sunday meetings.

It was early Sunday afternoon and David was going to be picking me up for church in about an hour. We'd agreed that he would join me at my ward today. I'd spent the morning reading my scriptures and asking Heavenly Father to help me to love David the way that a wife should. It was a beautiful February day, the sun was shining and some of the spring flowers were starting to poke their heads through the soil. It hadn't snowed in nearly two weeks. The weather was warm enough that I was dressed in a new spring outfit. I'd gone shopping the day before and found this beautiful sky blue skirt and an eggshell blouse to go with it. I'd spent far too much money but I felt that since it was my birthday, I deserved it. Adding a string of pearls, I looked at the result in the mirror. Perfect!

Ten minutes later as I was looking for smudges in my makeup, someone knocked at the door. Cindi answered it and then came looking for me.

"Sheryl, David's here. Are you going to go to church with us today or are you going to skip and go with him?" She was still upset and was almost accusatory in her question. I knew she didn't approve of my missing our ward to go to church with David. She was giving me another subtle hint.

"David and I are going to go to our ward today." I tried to smile back at her to make her feel at least a little guilty at accusing me falsely.

She didn't seem to notice. As she turned to go, she replied, "Well then, I'll see you there."

"Cin…" I blurted out and then hesitated, unsure of how to proceed. She paused and turned back around to look at me. I knew that I needed to say something but it wasn't going to be easy. I'd been wrong to treat her that way. She was my best friend.

"Yeah?" I could tell that she was still hurt by the look in her eyes. She shuffled from foot to foot and obviously didn't feel comfortable around me anymore.

"Listen, about earlier. I… I'm sorry. I just have been so confused recently about a lot of things and school's not going as well as I want and I took it out on you. Will you forgive me? I need a friend right now. I need someone to talk to and to help me with some decisions."

Cindi seemed to relax and leaned against the bathroom door. "Listen Sheryl, I know that you've got a lot on your mind and I shouldn't have been so rough on you but you're worrying me and the others. I'll always be here when you need me. Ok?"

I'd just put my mascara on and didn't want to have to redo it but I felt the tears coming so I quickly gave her a hug and said "Thanks Cin. You're always right on this kind of stuff. Can we talk this evening?"

"I'll be here. Anytime." She turned to go and then stopped, "By the way - you look great in that outfit! I don't suppose that I could borrow it sometime?"

I nodded as I took a big breath and held it, trying to keep from crying. Looking in the mirror, I noticed that a couple of drops had made it through and I dabbed at my eyes with a Kleenex before letting out a big sigh which seemed to do the trick. I wasn't going to cry after all. "Thanks, lets talk about it. I guess I should go see why David's here so early." Giving her another big hug, I walked down the hall and into the living room. David was there clearing off the end table near the lazy boy. He had dumped everything that had been there on the couch in a big heap.

"David. You're early!" Then noticing what he was doing I asked "What're you up to?"

Turning around at the sound of my voice he replied, "Well Peaches, I didn't want a birthday girl to quietly celebrate her birthday alone so I'm getting ready to give you your birthday present."

"How… When did you learn it was my birthday?" I must've spoken a little louder than I'd calculated and Cindi overheard.

"Sheryl? Is it your birthday?" Sheepishly I nodded. "Why didn't you tell us? I could've baked a cake and we could've had a little party. Now it's the Sabbath and I can't." I shrugged my shoulders secretly excited that someone' noticed and was happy for me.

David was smiling and indicating that I should close my eyes and sit down he said "That's ok Cindi, Sheryl's mom told me that Sheryl likes to pretend to suffer on her birthday so I'm not surprised that she didn't tell you. As for the party… perhaps there's still time, Sheryl, please go over on the couch and sit down with your eyes closed. Cin, can you help me here for a moment?"

"Sure, I guess I could." Her attitude about David seemed to be changing a little as he used some of his magic on her.

Sneaking a peak through my eyelashes I saw David heading for the front door. "Don't you go cheating on us Sheryl." Feeling guilty I closed them tight and mumbled that I wasn't looking. I heard the door open and then more than two sets of feet come into the house. Cindi gasped and let out a little squeak but David shushed her right away. I started to open my eyes to see what was going on but decided that I'd find out soon enough so I pinched them even tighter. After a moment the door closed, the extra feet had left, and all was silent.

After about five agonizing minutes I felt someone standing in front of me. I didn't actually reach out and touch them it was more like I could sense that the floor in front of me was no longer empty. Someone was there. I could sense their presence, their spirit. The position of the sensation changed and I directed my face downward toward a figure who was now kneeling in front of me. As if just on cue, David spoke from the floor immediately before me. "O.K. you can open your eyes now." I did and I was staring directly into his.

The deep blue of his eyes seemed to draw me closer until I was drowning. He was grinning with boyish abandon as he pulled a large bundle of pink carnations, from behind his back and pointing with them toward the end table said, "I hope you like it Peaches, I got it with us in mind but it's for your birthday." I looked over at the table just in time to see Cindi press a button on a huge stereo. Instantly the room was filled with the sounds of Kenny G.

Cindi was impressed. "Wow! Would you look at this stereo Sheryl? It's got everything. That's a DVD drive there so you can play movies as well as listen to your CDs. This sounds great!"

I looked back at David and I saw an eagerness, no a hunger there that yearned for recognition. I smiled and leaned toward him and gave him a quick kiss. "Thank you David. I guess that Mom told you when my birthday was. I usually try and forget it. I think though, that just this once, I'll ignore my inner voice and have some fun as I turn twenty-one."

"Are you that old? I thought you looked closer to eighteen." He teased "I'm glad that I'm not robbing the cradle as I'd originally thought. Happy birthday Peaches." He gave me another quick kiss and then pulled me up from the couch to dance with him for a few minutes before we had to go to church. I didn't seem to mind that he'd called me Peaches either. I'd grown accustomed to that name over the last few weeks as he ignored my increasingly weaker protests over its use. I decided that it was a little thing and I could let him have his way with that. I still felt uncomfortable with the way he said it but I figured that I'd get used to it. I guess I had.

Instead of going ahead alone, Cindi stayed back and went with us when it was time to go to church. As we walked over to David's car I felt a little light headed but holding onto David's arm I steadied myself and continued. David didn't seem to notice when I leaned on him a little more for support. I was surprised when David didn't just finger the alarm and move to his side of the car. Instead he opened my door and allowed Cindi to get in before handing me into the front seat. As I sat down, I thought *That's new. David's never opened my door for me. I wonder if it's just because it's my birthday or because he wants to make a good impression on Cindi.* Thanking him, I turned to fasten my seat belt as he got in and started the car. The drive was short and we were lucky in finding a parking place being vacated close to the building as we drove up. Parking there, David quickly got out and ran around the car to open my door. *It must be that he's trying for a good impression.* "Thank you David. It just occurred to me. You haven't met Bishop Thomas yet have you?"

His smile faltered a little and then reappeared as he quickly replied. "No, I haven't but I trust that you'll introduce me."

Taking his arm again I lead him toward the Tanner building for church. "I'd be happy to do so." As we started up the steps, I stumbled a little as my eyes glazed over and I nearly blacked out. David quickly caught me and kept me from falling.

Startled, Cindi said "Are you ok Sheryl?"

"Yes I think so. For some reason I felt a little faint. I'll be ok though. Thanks for keeping me on my feet David. Lets just go inside where I can sit down a little. I think I'll be ok then. It must be all of the excitement you two started back at the house." Starting forward again I paused after a few steps. "Guys, will you do me a favor?"

"Sure" the reply was in unison.

"Don't tell anyone else that it's my birthday. I really don't like it when people make a big thing out of it. O.K.?"

"No problem. My lips are sealed" Cindi winked as she moved past to open the door into the building.

"Sure thing Peaches." Taking my arm David helped me through the door and into a chair where sacrament meeting was getting ready to begin. Bishop Thomas saw us come in and started toward us as I sat down.

"Sheryl! It's good to see you again. We've missed your lovely voice the past few weeks but I understand from Cindi that you had a good reason for missing." Turning toward David, he held out his hand. "I understand that you're the reason for Sheryl's apparent inactivity. Congratulations on your engagement. You've been attending your ward haven't you?"

"Yes Bishop." David seemed fully at ease and the hint of apprehension that I'd seen earlier was totally gone. "This week we decided that it was time for me to attend Sheryl's ward."

"Well then - welcome. It's nice to have you here." Turning back to me, he asked. "Have you set a date yet for the wedding?" His eyes were warm and loving and I knew that he didn't really know about my indecision or David's and my agreement. As I opened my mouth to respond, David quickly replied.

"Not yet but I think that it'll be soon, probably this summer after Sheryl graduates. I've got another semester after that."

Bishop Thomas didn't miss the signs of a quick panic attack in me even though I tried to quell it as soon as I felt it coming. David was presuming too much and had encroached on our agreement. Now was not the time to discuss it though so I smiled back at David as he looked down at me with a little twinkle of triumph in his eyes. "Well that's great. Listen Sheryl. I'd like to talk with you. Could you come to my office on Tuesday afternoon at about 2:00?" Nodding that I could make it, I listened as he continued "Great then. I'll see you there and David, it was good meeting you. Please come again next week."

"Sure thing Bishop. Thanks for stopping to introduce yourself." As Bishop Thomas walked away, David sat down next to me and leaned closer to whisper in my ear as he squeezed my hand. "I'm sorry Peaches. I find myself replying that way when people ask. It just seems so awkward to have to answer 'we haven't set a date yet'. Forgive me?"

I didn't want to make a big deal about it and I *had* been thinking that if I were ever able to figure out my feelings that August would be a great time for a wedding. The Denver Temple grounds are so beautifully landscaped and full of flowers at that time. The weather's usually warm and sunny, a good time for a wedding. "Its ok. It just took me by surprise. I've been thinking though that sometime in August might not be a bad idea but I… " I wasn't ready for David's reaction.

"Are you serious! That's great! Hawaii'is so nice that time of year!"

"David, I didn't say that I was ready to set a date only that I was thinking about it as we'd agreed. What do you mean about Hawaii?"

"I'd thought that it would be nice to spend a couple of weeks there on our honeymoon. What do you think?"

"That sounds nice but lets get married first ok?"

"I guess that we could do that. Its been nearly three weeks. Do you think that we can talk about it after church today?"

In order to change the subject I nodded acceptance and then shushed him as Bishop Thomas stood to begin the meeting. "Brothers and Sisters, We'd like to begin by singing hymn number…"

It was nice being "home" in my own ward. I didn't feel like a stranger here and David seemed to enjoy the talks, at least his comments to me every once in a while were positive unlike when we attended his ward. He usually gave his own version of a talk on the subject as a whispered conversation to me. It generally annoyed me. Today was different. He was different. *Come to think about it, David's been too different.* I shivered as a cold chill ran up my spine at the thought. I dismissed it.

I felt distant though. The disorientation that I'd felt earlier came back and it felt as though the room was slowly circling, first to the left and then to the right. I tried to ignore the nausea that seemed to be building in my stomach by clenching my teeth but I knew that I was losing the battle. During the musical number before the last speaker I started to shiver again and feel flushed. Cindi sitting next to me noticed first. "Sheryl, are you ok? Do you need my jacket?"

Not wanting to unclench my teeth in order to speak I shook my head and leaned into David's arm. He looked down at me and smiled before putting his arm around me and pulling me closer. I didn't resist because it was warmer and for a few moments the shivers went away. By the time the final speaker was through I knew that I wasn't going to make it the rest of the way through the meetings and I decided that I'd go home. I'd caught a cold or the flu. As the congregation started singing the closing song I looked up at David and, pulling his sleeve, got his attention. "David, I'm not feeling very well. I think I've caught a cold. Would you take me home?" He nodded and gave me a little hug by pulling me closer for a moment. After the prayer I told Cindi that I wasn't feeling well and that David was going to take me home.

"Do you want me to come home with you?"

"No. Thanks though. I think I just have a cold so I'm going to take some orange juice and then get some rest."

"Ok then. I'll check on you when I get home."

"Thanks - maybe we can have that talk tomorrow instead?" My eyes pleaded with her. *I really do need to talk to you.* I'd decided that I wanted to hear her advice on what I needed to do about David. *No matter what you say.*

"Sure. Take care of yourself." Then she gave me a quick hug and turned to David. "Thanks for taking her home. There's some cold medication in the kitchen cabinet with my stuff. Give her a little before you leave"

"Thanks. I will."

David helped me out of the chapel, through the crowd of people, and then outside. I was glad that he'd found such a close parking space because I nearly fainted as he opened my door. I don't remember much of the short drive home. I just kept thinking to myself. *Don't be sick in David's car. It would never come out of the leather.* I gave David my keys and he helped me to the door. Once inside, he carefully helped me to the living room couch and then found a blanket from somewhere to put on me.

As I started to warm up under the blanket, David went over to the stereo and put on some soothing music. Turning around he spoke. "Cindi said that there was some cold medicine in the kitchen cabinet. Should I get some for you with a glass of orange juice?" My teeth wouldn't stop chattering so I nodded. He moved into the kitchen while he continued to talk. "This is a big dud, being sick on your birthday. Is there anything else that I can get for you?"

After a moment I managed to reply "N - N - No b-but thank y-you." Closing my eyes, I listened while he tinkered around in the kitchen looking through the cupboards for the medicine or a glass. I heard him mumble that he'd found one and then the refrigerator opened. "Boy! You girls sure do eat lean. I've never seen so much yogurt in my life. It looks like you're nearly out of orange juice though. I'll bring you some more, later this evening. I just went shopping last night and have a full gallon." I heard the tinkle of a liquid being poured into a glass and the refrigerator opened again. Ten seconds later David was kneeling on the floor beside me with a glass of orange juice and was helping me to sit up so that I didn't spill it. "Bottoms up. You'll need all of this if you hope to get better soon." Obediently I drank it down and then thanked him. "Do you want me to stay for a few minutes in case you need anything?"

"No. I'll be ok. I'm just going to go back into my bedroom and go to sleep. Thanks Bill, I really appreciate it. I'm sorry that this kind of messes up our plans for a talk."

"David."

"What?"

"My name's David not Bill." His voice was cool and calculating.

"Did I say Bill?" He nodded "I'm terribly sorry David. I'm so confused right now and ... well, I'm sorry."

"Sure. Well, let me help you to the hall at least." He helped me up from the couch and walked me toward the back of the apartment. I was grateful that he was here because I wasn't sure that I would've made it alone. Reaching the hallway he said "This is as far as I should go. Do you think you can make it the rest of the way on to your own?"

"Yes, mine's that one there." Indicating the closest door, "I would kiss you goodbye but under the circumstances I don't want to get you sick too. Would you close and lock the door when you leave?"

"Sure." He stayed in the hallway entrance until I'd made it to my room and then as I turned to wave goodbye to him he smiled and then left. I heard the music go off and then the door open and then close.

I was feeling really weird. *It must be the cold medicine.* I told myself. My head was spinning and I was getting warm and flushed as I moved toward my bed. My eyes were drooping by the time I changed into my night dress and climbed up onto my bed. The last thing I remember as I pulled my down comforter up to my chin is thinking *I forgot to turn off my desk lamp.*

9

"Cindi, what do you think I should wear tonight?"

Church was over and Heather and I were walking home. The afternoon had turned a little cool and the western sky had begun to fill with clouds ominously as if to signal that the short break from winter was over. I felt chilled for some reason besides the weather. My mind had been occupied by Sheryl ever since the start of Relief Society. I hadn't been able to concentrate on the lesson and for some reason I was nervous and tense. Heather on the other hand was animated and eagerly anticipating the evening's fireside at the Marriot Center. Chris, a decent looking guy in our ward, had asked her to go with him.

"What's wrong with what you have on?" She was conservatively dressed in the earthy tones that emphasized her Asian features. She'd been adopted by an LDS family when she was only days old. Her mother had been a victim of a violent act committed by an occupying force in her native land and, instead of opting for an abortion, had chosen to give her child up for adoption. Heather had never seen her native country, Viet Nam, but instead grew up a full-fledged American girl in Salt Lake. Now, she was beginning to feel a call toward her ethnic people and the needs of a small country struggling to rebuild itself after decades of political and economic turmoil. She'd just returned from the Los Angeles, Viet Namese speaking mission in August and had promptly added Viet Namese as a second major. Her degree in economics was almost finished and she hoped to somehow use the two areas of her education to improve the lives and education of her former country men.

"He's already seen me in it. I've been keeping an eye on Chris and want to see him again."

I rolled my eyes a little as we crossed campus drive near the law building. For a 'mature' woman, and a returned missionary, Heather sometimes struck me as being a little too air-headed. Sighing with exasperation I replied, "Honestly, Heather, what makes you think that what you wear is going to determine if he's going to ask you out again? Just be yourself. It's you that he wants to get to know, not your wardrobe."

"But I don't want him to think that I wear the same thing all day!"

I couldn't help but laugh, "Listen to your self, will you! You don't want him to think that you're like every other person on this planet who wears the same set of clothes all day. Now if you were wearing the same clothes everyday day in and day out *then* I'd be worried. Don't even bother. He won't even notice. He's more interested in you than anything else. I heard him talking in the hall with Jeff Daniels. He said that he couldn't believe you'd said yes when he asked. He said that he wished that he'd asked much sooner instead of waiting until there are only two months left in the school year."

Heather stopped. "He said that! *Now* I *have* to make sure I look awesome!"

Turning and motioning for her to continue walking I laughed as I said, "I should never have told you! Come on! Its starting to get cold and Sheryl went home sick after sacrament meeting. I want to make sure she's ok."

"OK. I wonder if she's contagious. I don't want to get sick tonight!" Shaking my head, I increased my pace a little so that we could make the light at the corner.

As we crossed the street and went into the parking lot around our condo, I looked for David's car. It wasn't there. Thinking to myself, *He must've dropped her off and then went home.* We started toward the stairs. For some reason, I began to shiver uncontrollably, then the wind picked up. We nearly ran the last thirty feet to the door because of the wind. There were small flakes of snow starting to trickle down from the darkening sky. As I put my key in the door to unlock it I noticed that it wasn't locked. *That's strange.* I thought. *Sheryl always locks the door when she's alone.* Opening the door, I went in.

Looking around I saw that there were a couple of blankets on the couch and a few dishes had been washed and placed on a dish towel to dry. Otherwise the house looked exactly like it did before Sheryl, David, and I had left for church. Taking off my jacket, I moved through the hall into my room to place it on my bed. That finished, I knocked lightly at Sheryl's door to see if she needed anything.

Getting no response, I quietly opened the door and found her sleeping on her back with her right foot sticking out from under the comforter. I quietly went to the bed and felt her head to see if she had a fever. She was a little cool and clammy but seemed to be sound asleep. Glancing at the clock radio on Sheryl's night stand, I saw that it was already 4:00. I'd skipped lunch earlier and now was feeling really hungry. As I turned to leave, Sheryl stirred and groaned as if she was having some kind of bad dream and was in discomfort. She rolled fitfully onto her side and pulled her knees up while mumbling. The movement had dislodged the comforter and the quilt that went on top of that. Quietly I replaced the bedding on top of her and then stepped back into the hall closing the door behind me.

Heather'd gone into her room and was taking out various articles of clothing from her closet and just as quickly discarding them on the bed. I stopped at her door and watched for a couple of seconds to see if she'd notice that I was there. After a minute I decided that if she ever found the 'right' outfit then Chris had better be careful. My stomach rumbled and gave me away. "Cindi, what do you think of this one?" She was holding a black-velvet dress with white lace around the collar up to herself and slowly turning from side to side as she looked into the full length mirror hanging on the closet door. It was the nicest dress I'd ever seen her wear.

"I think that if you wore that with a string of pearls and some of that new perfume that you bought the other day then you'll be engaged within two weeks and married by the end of the summer."

"Are you serious?" She looked at me as though she were gauging my answer. Then as if she'd come to a conclusion she continued seriously. "I don't have any pearls."

Laughing I walked in and took the dress from her and holding it up to her size four frame I acted as though I was deep in thought. Heather stopped her fidgeting and was eagerly looking into my face, awaiting the decision she sensed was coming. Breathing in quickly and pursing my lips I shook my head resolutely. "Yep, this is the one. Use the black shoes there and a pair of black nylons with this dress and he's got no hope of ever getting away with one date. As for the pearls, I'll loan you mine if you promise to take extra care of them. I got them from my grandmother before she passed away. They've always brought me luck. I think that you'll find them lucky too." Handing the dress to her, I turned to go. "Wait here and I'll get them for you." She nodded and then turned back to the mirror to examine the dress again.

As I moved past Sheryl's room, I heard her mumbling. Retrieving the pearls I gave them to Heather and then went to check on Sheryl again. She was tossing back and fourth on the bed and was curled up in fetal position holding her stomach moaning. She'd kicked off the covers and as I turned around from flipping the desk lamp on I saw it. "Sheryl are you ok? Sheryl?!" I was alarmed and yelled out to Heather. "Heather! Get in here quickly, I think something's wrong with Sheryl!" I quickly went to the bathroom and grabbed a towel and placed it on the bed to cover the worst of it as Sheryl rolled over onto it. Because of the towel, Heather didn't see the spots of blood when she first came in. I had Sheryl's head in my arms and was slowly rocking her back and fourth whispering softly to her. After a few minutes she calmed down a little but the mumbling continued. She still seemed to feel most comfortable in fetal position.

"What's going on?" Heather still hadn't caught onto what was happening. Then she saw the stains on Sheryl's night dress and her hand went quickly to her mouth in shock. "Is she having her period? Why's she still asleep?"

"I don't know and that's what's bothering me. About two weeks ago she came into my room to borrow some napkins because she'd run out so I assumed that she was having it then. If that was true then she shouldn't be bleeding now. I think something's terribly wrong. Please help me with her. Can you get a wet cloth from the bathroom and we'll see if we can wake her up?" A cold chill went through me as I thought about the earlier feeling that I'd during Relief Society. *"Check on Sheryl."* I'd rationalized my inaction to myself by saying that I was going to see her in thirty minutes. It had come once more after the closing prayer. *"Check on Sheryl. Go now."* I'd found Heather and we'd left right away for home. Looking at the clock on the night stand I thought.

That was only twenty minutes ago. What happened? As I sat there and held Sheryl's head I stroked her hair and my tears flowed freely as I prayed. *Heavenly Father, please help me. Something's wrong with Sheryl and I don't know what to do. Help me to be able to be there for her. Guide my hands. What can I do?*

As I sat there, a thought came clearly to my mind. *"Call your home teachers. Give her a blessing."* Heather returned with the cloth and gave it to me before speaking. "We need to call someone." I nodded.

"Go next door and see if Tim and Doug are home from church yet. If so, have them come quickly to give her a blessing. I'll stay here and keep trying wake her up." Heather turned quickly and ran for the door. I heard it open and felt the cold wind blowing into the house but didn't hear it close. As I waited, I surveyed the room. Sheryl's skirt and blouse were neatly draped across the chair by the desk and her books were stacked perfectly on the corner of the desk. A picture of her family was framed in a nice silver frame hanging over the desk. Near the door hung a small photo of the Salt Lake Temple with a beautiful orange sunset behind it, next to that hung a picture of Christ. His eyes seemed to be directed at us sitting on the bed. Nothing seemed out of place or wrong except that Sheryl was bleeding and wouldn't wake up. Realizing that it wouldn't be too long before Tim and Doug came over and had to come in here to give her a blessing I started looking for something that I could put around Sheryl to cover her up. My eyes fell on the comforter and blanket that had fallen on the floor. Reaching over I grabbed a corner of the blanket and pulled it over to me just as I heard the door close and then Heather talking with someone.

Heather came in and, seeing that I was trying to cover Sheryl up, quickly helped and then surveyed the room for something. Seeing that Sheryl had left her bra on the dresser, she quickly put it in the top drawer before nodding to herself. "I'll get the elders now." Poking her head through the door, she called "Tim? Doug? It's ok now. Please come on back. We can't bring her out there."

Someone replied "O.K."

Seconds later Tim poked his head through the door tentatively before coming in. He was dressed in a white shirt and blue dockers. His silk tie was loosened at the collar and the wind had blown his sandy hair out of place. He looked at Sheryl and then at me. "What's going on? Heather said that Sheryl was sick?" At the sound of his voice Sheryl moaned loudly and started rocking back and fourth again. She seemed to be agitated.

Moving my mouth to her ear I rocked her as I whispered to her "Shhh - its ok. Tim and Doug are here to give you a blessing. I'll be right here and so will Heather. Heavenly Father told me that you needed this." Her arm moved toward mine until her hand was touching my forearm. As I continued to rock with her and whisper to her she began to relax and slowly after a couple of minutes she stopped moaning and seemed to relax completely. I nodded to Tim as Doug moved through the doorway past Heather. "Thanks Tim. She went home early from church because she was ill. I just found her and I think…" As I was speaking a very solid thought came into my mind. *"Something's wrong and you're doing exactly what she needs. After this, get her to the hospital to see a doctor."* I didn't realize that I'd stopped talking until Doug spoke.

"You think something's wrong?"

Nodding through the wave of tears that had come with the thought, I tried to continue. "I know something's wrong. There's a feeling here that isn't right. I know she needs a blessing. She won't wake up. She just lays here like this and moans and tosses around. She's also bleeding." As I finished Tim and Doug looked at each other and then back at me with confusion in their eyes. They looked at Sheryl again and then nodded. I tried to explain. "She shouldn't be bleeding this time of the month. Please, let's give her a blessing and then I need to get her to see a doctor." They both nodded as understanding replaced confusion.

"I'll go get my car and start it warming up as soon we finish with the blessing. You can get her dressed in something else, if you need to, before we take her."

"Thanks Tom. Do you need me to move so that you can give her the blessing?"

Shaking his head, he moved toward the desk and the left side of the bed. "No. I'll stand here where I can reach her head. Doug will stand beside me." Looking at Doug he asked "Doug, will you anoint her?"

"Sure"

Doug moved toward the bed hesitantly and nervously lifted a small vial toward Sheryl's head. His hands were smooth and well manicured and for a moment I thought I saw a white light surround them and they blurred a little bit as if they were morphing into someone else's hands. *Probably the effect of the tears in my eyes.* I thought. "Does she have a middle name?"

"I don't know. Does it matter?"

With a timid voice he replied. "No, the Lord knows whom He's blessing." I was struck by this as I thought to myself. *This is a man worthy of the priesthood. He knows that he's not blessing Sheryl but the Lord is!* I nodded and hugging Sheryl's head to my chest I kissed it before closing my eyes.

Doug placed his hands on Sheryl's head and began "Sister Sheryl Summerhayes, by the power of the Holy Melchezidek priesthood... In the name of Jesus Christ, Amen." His voice had changed. It was confident, and strong, not demanding but completely different from the voice that he normally used. Tim moved closer and his hands joined Doug's and he began the blessing.

"Sister Sheryl Sommerhayes,... I seal this anointing and give you a blessing...The consequences of the choices others make will be rewarded on their heads by the Lord in the His due time...Be a true follower of Christ...This blessing, and all others that you stand in need of, I seal on your head, Amen."

As Tim finished, Sheryl relaxed completely and seemed to sleep even more deeply. Looking up toward Tim and Doug I could barely see their faces through my own tears. "Thanks" was all I could say. The spirit in the room had changed completely.

Wiping at his eyes, Tim nodded and in a voice deep with emotion he looked me in the eyes and said "Cindi, the Lord showed me what happened." Doug was crying unabashedly and nodded. "Sheryl needs you very much and will need you even more in the future. Get her to the doctor as soon as possible. I'll go get the car." Looking at Heather he said through a rising torrent of tears. "Don't do anything with the bed linens. Don't touch anything in this room. Call Bishop Thomas and tell him that he's needed immediately at the hospital." He then turned and ran out of the house for his car. Doug followed. Heather and I looked at each other in confusion.

As I gathered a few things for Sheryl I thought back on what Tim had said in the blessing. *"You'll be comforted by the friends that you've made in your efforts to live the gospel of Jesus Christ...Your body is injured and your spirit seeks comfort. These wounds will heal with the love of your Father in Heaven who knows you individually and has a great work for you to do...The choices we make in this life are ours and your Father in Heaven must allow us and others to make those choices even if they bring pain to others...Your pain will be lessened through your diligence in seeking the scriptures and the gospel of Jesus Christ."* My mind raced tying to figure out what had happened to

Sheryl. *Why'd she need such a powerful blessing right now?* A few moments later Tim came back and helped me get Sheryl down to his car for the ride to the hospital.

10

Thirty minutes ago Tim had carried Sheryl, still unresponsive and in some discomfort, into the emergency room of the Utah Valley Regional Medical Center. The triage nurse had instantly recognized a need for immediate attention and had led us back to a small curtained alcove off of the ER nurses' station. Tim had gone out to park his car and wait for Bishop Thomas to arrive. I stayed with Sheryl and waited for the doctor to come. As I waited, I prayed. *Father, please help me to listen next time I am told by the spirit to do something. If I had listened the first time then I might have been home to stop whatever happed to Sheryl. Please give me the strength to be there for Sheryl. Help me to be able to handle the truth and be a support to her.* I had begun to suspect that something unthinkable had happened. I was denying my feelings right now - waiting for a doctor or someone else to say it first.

As I looked down at Sheryl lying there on the hospital bed in her night shirt with a blanket wrapped around her, I started to cry again. *Oh Sheryl, why couldn't it have been me? Why did it have to be you?* The triage nurse had checked Sheryl briefly when we had come in and told me that the bleeding had stopped but that I was right to bring her in. Now nearly thirty minutes later I was not sure if I believed her. Sheryl was starting to toss and turn more often now and seemed to realize that she was not at home anymore.

Just as I was about to get up and call a nurse, the doctor arrived. "Hi, you must be Cindi, I know this young lady is Sheryl. I am Dr. Christine Thurman. Tell me what happened as far as you know."

I told her about Sheryl getting sick at church and going home. I told her about finding the door unlocked when I got home after church. The horror of discovery came back to me as I described what I first saw. I was somehow detached from myself as I described the things we had tried to wake her, how we had used a cool cloth on her head or gently shaking her and yelling her name. I told her how Sheryl was doubled over and groaning and moaning in some kind of discomfort. I told her everything I could remember.

As I was talking, Dr. Thurman was taking some notes and examining Sheryl. The duty nurse came in about five minutes later. When I finished, Dr. Thurman turned to the nurse and gave her orders. She wanted some blood tests done and another examination room prepared. After the nurse left, she turned to me. "Cindi, you did the right thing in bringing her here. I think I know what is wrong with her and why she won't wake up. If I am right and the blood tests prove to be positive then you have nothing to worry about. Sheryl will wake up in about two hours." As I breathed a big sigh of relief, she shook her head negatively and continued, "If I am right, then waking up will be one of the most difficult things she will have to face. Now I need to ask some questions and I need some honest answers. I would prefer to ask Sheryl and I will eventually have to do so but I need to know some things before I can continue with my examination." I nodded indicating that I would answer them as best as I could. "They may not be pleasant questions."

I swallowed hard and then nodded again "Ok. I'll tell you what I can."

"When was Sheryl's last menses?" I told her about Sheryl borrowing supplies from me about two weeks ago. She nodded and continued "That is probably a good assumption - we will run with that until I can talk with Sheryl. You told me that you are both LDS right?"

"Yes."

"Are you both active and committed to the gospel and its teachings?" I was a little confused, wondering why the doctor would ask about something like this when Sheryl was lying there on the bed but I responded affirmatively. "Now, one last question, do you know if Sheryl is sexually active in any way?"

"No!" I yelled, totally shocked that she would ask. Then, realizing that I had yelled, I continued in a near whisper "I mean I know that she is not. We talked about it only a few days ago. She was getting nervous because she was engaged and was a little scared of what was going to happen on her wedding night. We talked girl talk and stuff. I know that she would not have lied about something like that." Suddenly my mind put the pieces together. Sheryl was bleeding when she shouldn't. She was cramping and in pain and the doctor was asking about Sheryl and whether she had ever had sex before. I started to shake and tremble as I saw confirmation in the doctor's eyes even as I asked "She has been raped hasn't she?"

Dr. Thurman nodded her head and said "Until I can talk to her I have to assume that is the case. It may still turn out that she consented to this but the condition that she is in now with the unresponsiveness is an indication that this may have been non-consensual and aided by the use of a drug of some kind. The blood work will verify that. My examination indicates that sometime within the last 12 hours she has been penetrated for the first time. That is the source of the blood that caused your concern. It will heal in a few days. There are bodily fluids still present and if her period was a little more than two weeks ago then we may have a more lasting result. She may become pregnant though it appears that whom ever it was, used some kind of 'protection'. I have ordered examination room one prepared so that I can collect any evidence that may still be present in a private room while trying to maintain her privacy. When she wakes up, the police will want to talk to her but she will need you and perhaps a close family friend or relative. Can you make some calls?"

Totally numb I nodded that I would as two orderlies were let into the area by Dr. Thurman and wheeled Sheryl out and into a private room. We followed and then Dr. Thurman shut the door. "She will be ok for a few minutes. I understand that you have people in the waiting room. Would you like me to come out and talk with them or would you like to do it? You can use the small chapel off of the waiting room for a little privacy."

"Thanks, I'll tell them."

I was numb and in shock. I had heard of things like this happening and even seen a talk show on television the other day. The women on the show had all been traumatized years ago and some were still living with nightmares about it. As I looked down at Sheryl, my eyes filled with tears. She is such a good person. Why did this have to happen to her? How could it happen here at BYU? Then a more chilling thought came to me. *It did happen and here at BYU, in your very own apartment!* My knees began to shake and I started to collapse. I am not sure how I managed to get to the sink before I retched, but I did. Nothing came though my guts churned and heaved. After a few moments I was feeling a little better but the reality of the situation had settled onto my shoulders like a giant cloud. I could barely breathe. As I leaned against the sink, I sobbed uncontrollably.

......

It was nearly twenty minutes later, after I had composed my self, that I went out to meet Tim and Bishop Thomas. Doug, Heather and her date Chris had arrived by that time too. They were pacing and anxious. Seeing me come out of the automatic doors, with my eyes all puffy and red and shuffling along using the wall to keep my balance, did not do anything to make them feel much better. I ignored their eyes, not wanting to see the questions that they held. Instead I moved toward the admission's desk and quietly asked directions toward the chapel. Hearing the interchange, Bishop Thomas took my arm and led me toward the room just down the hall. As we reached the door I turned to the others and said, "Could I have a moment with Bishop Thomas first? I promise that I will let you know what is going on as soon as possible. Sheryl is ok and only sleeping. She will wake up in the next hour or two according to the doctor. When she does" I had to stop and swallow hard before continuing. "I need to be with her." I had thought that all of my tears had been shed but as I stumbled through the last little bit my stomach lurched into my throat and I had to choke back a sob. Tears trickled down my cheeks as they all quietly nodded and Bishop Thomas solemnly conducted me into the chapel.

After the door had been closed, we sat down and for a few minutes we said nothing. Bishop Thomas is a great man and he understood that I needed to be the one to speak first. So, as I sought to control my emotions, he took a seat across from me and folded his arms quietly. Slowly I was able to tell him that a nightmare had just begun for Sheryl. As I looked up after telling him what Dr. Thurman had said his eyes were wet and full of pain and I felt some relief from my burden.

"Cindi, I don't know how Sheryl is going to get through this but I know that she will need us more now than we have ever imagined. I have not had any training in this but there are a few books and bits of council that I have received over the years that will help us. Sheryl will not trust anyone, particularly a man, for some time. She will become depressed and even in her distrust she will not want to be alone. She will have sudden mood swings and at times she will rage at and hate the world for this cruel event. Through all of this we have to show her that we care and love her. We have to prove to her that she can trust us.

This will take a long time and we will need the Lord on our side. Tim warned me that he suspected something like this. He told me what happened when he and Doug gave Sheryl a blessing. I trust in that blessing. The Lord has Sheryl in his arms even now as we speak, comforting her." He paused and choked back his emotions before continuing. "As soon as she is willing to meet with me, I need you to bring her to me. We can get her some counseling and see that she gets the medical attention she needs. We also need to let her make the decision to call her family and tell them. That may be the most difficult part. I will take what action is needed with the University to see that she isn't victimized again in her schoolwork. I'll see that you also have the time and freedom to do what you need for her." I nodded. Somehow I was feeling better, more sure of myself and more capable of handling what was to come. "If you would like, I can ask Tim and Doug to assist me in giving you a blessing before you go back in to be with Sheryl."

"Please, I feel the Lord is helping but I also feel so confused and lost."

"Ok then, I will go call the others in and we will give you a blessing. I will then deal with them as you go back in to be with Sheryl. For now we will need to contain the news of what has happened to only the few of us until Sheryl is able to make a decision on how she wants to handle this. We don't want her victimized by rumors or half truths. We especially don't want her to have to endure the snickers and taunts of those that might not understand. Even LDS people can be insensitive sometimes." Moving to the door he opened it and motioned the others in. Heather came in first and knelt beside me and gave me a big hug. Her eyes were dark with fear as she took my hand in hers. I patted her hand and told her that it would be ok. Bishop Thomas took Tim and Doug aside and was talking quietly with them. Chris moved over to my other side and took my other hand in his.

"Are you ok? Heather told me that you were the one to find Sheryl."

Through a couple of sobs I assured him that I would be ok and then Bishop Thomas was there with my home teachers to give me a blessing. When it was over, I felt as though a warm blanket had been wrapped around me and I just had to hug everyone. Then, looking at Bishop Thomas I said. "Thanks, I need to get back to Sheryl. Let me know what you decide." Then I stood up and walked back to be with Sheryl when she woke up.

......

I woke up confused and disoriented on finding myself in the hospital. If Cindi had not been there, I don't know what I would have done. As it turned out I was glad to have her there when the Doctor came in and explained everything to me. I told her that I didn't remember anything and that she must be mistaken. As I looked into her eyes and saw the truth there I wanted to die. I couldn't cry. I couldn't feel anything. *How? Who? Why?* Then it started to

sink in. *I am soiled! All my life I have waited even when it was so tempting to give in.*
Now I never even got to make that choice and I am spoiled. Who is ever going to want me
now? I'll never get married! Then my mind went numb.

The Doctor said that my blood tests had shown evidence of a drug
called flunitrazepam. She told me it was a drug used as a sedative in Europe for
sleeping disorders and recently it had taken on a more sinister use in the United
States where it was illegal. Rohypnol, a trade name, was known as the 'date rape
drug' because it leaves the user sleepy and unable to control themselves. In
many cases they simply pass out leaving the way open for physical abuse. A
form of amnesia is also typical. In my case Dr. Thurman thought that the
alcohol in the cold medicine as well as the medication itself enhanced the effect
of the drug causing me to become unresponsive and resulting in the condition
that brought me to the hospital. She also explained that I was a little anemic
and that perhaps the anemia in combination with the drugs had also caused a
temporary change in my blood chemistry so that it did not clot as quickly as it
should. This is what had provided the signs that had alerted Cindi to my need.

This isn't happening to me. I just got sick and had a reaction to the cold medicine
that David gave me. I wasn't raped. By whom? I don't remember a thing! How could I
forget something like that? Even as I was telling myself it was a whole mistake my
body was telling me with its pains and cramping that they were right. Confused
now, and a little scared, I spoke. "But I didn't take any pills. I took the cold

medicine but that was a liquid." *This is unreal. Why aren't I crying. I should be crying.*

Dr. Thurman nodded and then replied. "Did you have any soft drinks or juice?"

I tried to remember but nothing seemed clear. After several minutes I had to admit that I couldn't remember. A rising surge of panic was quickly taking over my reason. I started shaking and getting light headed. Cindi held me and cried. *What are you crying about?* I thought *I should be crying! I am the one that was raped. Raped !!* As the thought sunk in and the reality dawned in my mind I screamed and then began to cry. *Finally!*

Later, as the police were questioning me, I was glad that Cindi was there. She was able to answer most of their questions while I slipped deeper into a growing depression that would eventually last for months, though it was deepest two weeks after I was allowed to return from the hospital.

The police found David's fingerprints on the desk lamp in my room and on one of the glasses in the kitchen. Faced with these pieces of evidence and some others that the police and the district attorney did not discuss with me, David eventually admitted to giving me the drug in a glass of orange juice but he denied ever touching me. He claimed that he had given it to me to help me to sleep and to rest.

He admitted turning off the lamp, claiming that he had gone out to the car and discovered that he had forgotten his keys. Returning to the apartment he had knocked and then called with no response. Fearing that I had fallen or something, he said that he had checked on me. Seeing that I was asleep and had left the desk lamp on, he turned it off. Because I could not remember anything that could prove that something else had happened and because there wasn't any additional physical evidence, the charge of rape against David had to be dropped. He was still punished for possession of a controlled substance and had to pay a very sizable fine. BYU suspended him and he was forced to move out of his apartment into a county correctional facility for ninety days.

Shortly after I had come home from the hospital, Bishop Thomas called to see how I was doing. I told him that I was fine but still a little uncertain about things but that it wasn't anything I couldn't handle. I don't know why I told him that. It was exactly the opposite of what I was feeling. I knew though that if I told him something else he would want to meet with me and I couldn't bring myself to do that. I couldn't be alone with a man even in what I knew would be a completely safe environment. Still it was comforting to know that every week he would call, sometimes two or three times. I always felt better after talking with him. Still I couldn't make an appointment.

My mind tormented me with thoughts that became more true and real with each time they floated to the top of the cesspool that had become my life, thoughts like - *What am I good for anymore? I can't go to the Temple or serve a mission anymore. No one will want me as a mother for their children. Children! I can't even tell my own children to wait until they are married! I am not worthy. Not after what happened. No one will ever want me.*

I was afraid to go to sleep. When I eventually did get to sleep I was tormented with nightmares and woke up screaming. I started shaking if I came home and someone other than one of my room mates was in the house. Cindi had traded rooms with me so that I didn't have to sleep in the same room every night. We thought that this would get rid of the nightmares but it didn't. I was slowly falling behind in my classes even as February wilted away and March sprouted, blossomed, and began to dim. Cindi was the only constant in my life. She was there every time I woke up screaming. She visited my classes and collected my homework on the days that I was too tired or frightened to get out of bed. She fended off the phone calls and questions that began soon after I had come home.

One afternoon, when everyone was going to class, I lied that I wasn't feeling well and therefore did not want to go with them. After they all left I locked the door and went into the kitchen to make a sandwich.

I set out all of the ingredients and dishes that I would need and sat down to prepare my lunch. Glancing around I noticed that I had forgotten a knife to cut some slices of cheese for my ham and cheese extravaganza. As I reached for a knife my arm froze. I couldn't will it to pick up the knife even as the though came into my mind. *"You can't live like this. You are a scared rabbit with splotchy fur. No one wants you. No one will ever want you the way you are. You are spoiled forever. End it. End it now!"*

"No" I whispered.

"Yes, You are worthless. You have nothing to live for. Your family will blame you for forsaking their teachings. You weren't married!"

Crying now I began to shake as I argued *"They will not. They love me no matter what happens."*

"They did but now you have shown them what kind of a person you are. You have shown them the truth about yourself." I hadn't noticed when the dark and clammy presence had entered the room but it was there now. There was a sense of anticipation and impending triumph that was almost tangible. *"Go on. There is the knife. You can end this pain, this torment. No one will be here for a long time. You can do it now and never have to worry that you will be rescued. No one cares anyway. You know I am right. You are spoiled forever. Not one person is going to love you now."*

Screaming in my mind I yelled "No!!" Then in a whisper I begged as I fell to the floor convulsing in fear. "Heavenly Father, Help me! I know that I am not worthy but please help me."

The phone rang even as the oppression lifted. After a few rings I pulled myself up and went to answer it. It was a doctor from LDS social services. Bishop Thomas had referred me to her and she wanted to set up an appointment with me. I started to say that I didn't need to talk with a counselor but then I remembered what had just happened and I asked how soon I could see her. She had an appointment immediately and invited me to come and talk. I got the information from her on where I needed to go and then hung up.

Dr. Smithson just listened to me and encouraged me to see things differently. It felt good to talk about it so I started going to see her twice a week. On one occasion, in late march, she helped me to think through some of my major problems. "Sheryl, you did nothing wrong. You have broken no laws, civil or spiritual, especially spiritual. Your Father in Heaven loves you just the same. Do you understand me?"

"I guess. But why do I feel so worthless? Why am I feeling guilty? Why can't I cry anymore? Surely there is something I did that makes it partly my fault? Was I giving some incorrect or improper signals? All I remember about that day was that I wasn't feeling well and I had leaned on him (I couldn't even say his name) a little more than I usually did. Did that mean that I was signaling him that it was ok?"

"Oh heavens Sheryl, none of that makes it your fault. You did nothing wrong, nothing that you aught to feel guilty over. Have you talked with Bishop Thomas yet?"

"We talk every week."

"When was your last appointment with him?"

"I ... uh ... I don't have any appointments with him."

"But you said that you talk with him every week."

"He calls me. I am too afraid to be alone with him."

"Is there something about Bishop Thomas that makes you afraid? Why would you not want to meet with him?"

"Well, He is one of them isn't he." At seeing the confusion on her face I felt that I needed to make it clearer. "He is a HE after all. Isn't he?"

"You mean he is a man." I nodded. "Are you afraid of all men?"

I hadn't thought of that. As I looked deeply into my feelings I realized that I had been avoiding everyone, even my own Father. Mom and Dad knew something was wrong and they called regularly but I hadn't told them what had happened. *How can I? They will disown me.* I couldn't face them with my shame. Slowly I nodded.

"Sheryl, you have been hurt. This is a natural feeling that you are experiencing. It is one that should be temporary. If it isn't and you are not able to get past it then you will be scarred for life. Do you understand?"

"Yes, but how? How can I ever feel safe again?"

"That's the issue isn't it? You don't feel safe around men because of what one individual has done."

"I guess it is."

"Sheryl, are there any men that you feel you could trust? Your family, Your father or maybe your brother? Is there someone that you can feel comfortable being around?"

"I ... I don't know. I suppose that somewhere there is someone that I could be safe with but I just don't know."

"Think about that Sheryl. Come back next week and let's talk about it again. Right now you don't feel safe with anyone but Cindi, your room mate, and it is making you miserable isn't it?"

She was right. I missed being able to go to the movies or just to sit and study in the library without feeling hunted. "Yes. I don't like to rely on Cindi so much but I don't know what I would do without her."

"I know Sheryl. Cindi has been a great friend. Now you need to break the ice and renew some of your other friendships. Broaden your circle of safety a little. Let one more person into your space this week. Let Cindi know that there is someone else that can also help share the burden. When you do this you will find that your depression and your insecurities will slowly begin to dissolve away and you will feel better and you will get over this. That's what you want isn't it?"

"I guess it is. Thanks." I got up as if to go.

"Oh! There is one more thing that can help you." Her voice had cracked and had an edge of deep emotion in it.

Interested, I sat down again. Nodding for her to continue I barely could believe what I was hearing.

"Sheryl, many women have been in the same position as you. Most all of them are able to deal with the issues and get over the trauma and live happy and fulfilled lives. You would be surprised but I know many women, LDS women, who have been through what you have been through and are now living happy and well adjusted lives with their husbands, their Eternal husbands." She paused and looked deeply at me, a small tear edging out the brown of her eyes. She continued "Yes, their Eternal husbands. They have gone to the temple and have been married there. They continue to go. They live worthy and guilt free lives."

I whispered my thought before I realized it. "Their husbands still want them even after what has happened?"

Dr. Smithson nodded. "Yes Sheryl, their husbands do want them and love them." Her eyes were full of tears now. "I know. I have been where you are today. I was older than you and I had already been married and I didn't know my attacker but that didn't make it any easier for me than it is for you. What I am trying to say is that I will be here if you need help. I know how you feel. I want you to know that even after what has happened to you, I want you as a friend. I would trust you with my own children."

I couldn't say anything. I was not ready to believe that there was any good left in me. There was a long pause and then she continued. "Many of us who have been though this have found that it is often helpful to write a letter expressing our feelings and our rage at what has been visited on us. We write to our assailants and vent our poisoned emotions on them. It helps, believe me. Some of us even have the courage to send those letters. Imagining them reading it and feeling our rage and hurt does something. It cleanses us. We find that we can face another day because we, in some way, have visited our horror back on our attacker forcing them to take some responsibility for their actions. If you think you can, try doing that. It really does help. It helps us to separate ourselves from them and helps our minds deal with the need to become productive in society again." With that she hugged me and I left to find Cindi waiting for me in the waiting room. Together we went home.

Several days later I was feeling bitter and angry and I decided to try what Dr. Smithson had suggested. I wrote a letter.

David,

I don't remember ever feeling more helpless as I did on hearing that you had given me that horrid drug. I know in my heart that you did something besides turn off my desk lamp. I don't have the ability to prove it though. I will work the rest of my life if necessary to prove that you have taken from me something beyond price. I feel violated and used. I had trusted you and had even decided that I loved you. I was eager to become your wife and was ready to set a date with you for our wedding. Now I feel nothing but loathing for you. I know that someday, the Lord will call you to account for your actions. Don't ever expect me to defend you. I will be the first witness against your actions. Don't ever come near me again.

Sheryl.

P.S. I am not a thief so here is your ring. I could have taken it, sold it and lived for a year on the money but I would much rather just throw it in the sewer where you belong. Also if you get out soon enough you just might be able to recover the stereo from my trash dumpster. They pick up the refuse on Friday mornings.

I took his ring, which I had thrown in the back of my closet, and put it in the envelope and gave it to Cindi. She told me she would see that David received it wherever he was. She told me later that she had bent the ring nearly flat before giving it to him. For some reason I felt better.

Several days later, feeling more liberated than I had in a long time I told Cindi that I wanted to try and go to my classes alone. I wanted to see if I could manage by myself. Cindi was worried and almost said something but paused and then nodded wearily.

If I knew beforehand what would happen I probably would not have ventured out. As it is, I am glad that things turned out the way that they did. Running into Bill changed everything.

11

When I first saw Bill I wanted to run but he was just lying there on the floor in a daze and I felt bad that it had been me that put him there. I hadn't been watching where I was going. Instead I had been thinking to myself that it had been a terrible idea to try and go to my classes alone. Every time I walked by a guy I flinched. The most recent encounter had been three large football players arrayed across the hall. I had cowered in the corner of a classroom doorway until they had passed, oblivious to my presence. In a panic I had thought, *I have to get home to Cindi. It isn't safe here. Please Heavenly Father, Help me.* I was practically running when Bill turned the corner and we hit.

As I helped him up from the floor with the assistance of some girl that seemed to be nearby I found myself thinking in fragments. *He ... looks good! ... lost weight ... Must have hurt his head ... makes him look healthier.* As I studied him for a few moments I remembered our trip to Colorado together. A slight smile came to my face. Then I remembered that he had been there when David had played that cruel and manipulative trick in front of my parents. My embryonic smile vanished in a flood of despair. *Why me? Why!! Can't I have any good memories without David intruding? I wish things were different. Bill would never have done that to me. Why couldn't he have been the one to take me home that afternoon? Why couldn't it have been Bill that I was going to marry? Now he will never want me!*

Realizing that my thoughts were moving in a direction I was not comfortable with I blushed a little as I lifted his arm to assist him in standing. I was glad that Bill seemed to be too dazed to have noticed. *That sure is a great cologne he is wearing. Stop it Sheryl! You have no choice. Don't ruin his life with your problems!* As Bill stumbled to his feet I quickly let go and, feeling a little unsteady myself, I stepped back and reestablished the barrier that I had learned to set up around my feelings.

Bill introduced me to Teri and then moved over to sit down on a bench. Teri and I talked for a few minutes and then I turned to go on to my class. Not wanting to seem callous or cold, I went over to the bench to say goodbye to Bill.

When he asked about my ring I wanted to die. My knees started to buckle and I just knew that I was going to faint. Teri kept me from falling down even as Bill reached to grab my hand in his. I hadn't cried in a long time. For some reason, Dr. Smithson had told me, my mind was not ready to deal with the next level of healing and because of that my tears were locked up. I had tried earlier. I had worked up my anger but that didn't work because the tears never came and I just felt worse. Now, when I didn't want them to come I couldn't stop them. My mind had found its time to release the flood gates and

I started to cry. Bill moved over and helped me to sit down next to him and he put his arms around me and just held me while I cried.

My mind was screaming *Sheryl, He is a man! Don't let him near you!* My heart ignored it and I snuggled closer and continued to cry on Bill's shoulder. He didn't say anything. He only held me close and rocked me back and forth slowly, his hand brushing the back of my head in slow and gentle strokes. Slowly, over time, my mind caught up with my heart and I felt safe for the first time in months. I realized that even before David had raped me I had not felt safe with him. I shuddered to think that for nearly six months I had dated someone that I didn't feel safe with. I had always felt defensive and unsure of myself when I was with David. Now, in the arms of Bill, I felt safe once again just like I had on our drive to Colorado.

Now my mind told me I could quit crying but I didn't want to. My heart was leapfrogging ahead again and I was crying because Bill was being so gentle. I didn't want it to end. Hesitantly I moved my head from his shoulder and looked into his eyes. They were deeply pained and conflicted. I knew I needed to say something but his lips began to move first.

"Sheryl, I ...I am sorry. I should never have intruded on you that way. I was shocked to see you and to see that your ring was gone. The last thing I wanted to do was to hurt you. I am so sorry." His hand went slowly to my head and he brushed the hair out of my face and brushed the tears from my cheek. Then he pulled me closer and pressed my head to his shoulder. "I have dreamt of ways to part you from that ring. I am sorry to see that whatever did it has been so traumatic for you. I am sorry." With that he kissed the top of my head and was silent.

My heart leapfrogged again as I realized that Bill cared. He was here comforting me. His thoughts right now were for me. He cared! My mind started to crawl slowly out of the abyss that I had been trapped in for so long. My heart tossed it a rope to safety and then realization came. I knew that I could trust Bill. I had found one more person besides Cindi that I could trust. Dr. Smithson was right. I could get over this. Quietly I thanked my Heavenly Father for letting me have such wonderful friends.

A few minutes later I gently pushed away from Bill. He let me go tenderly and in a very quiet, almost choked, voice he started to speak. "Sheryl, I am sor..." I didn't let him finish. Leaning over I kissed him on the cheek.

Pulling back I smiled. His cheek had been wet and a little salty. He had been crying with me. My mind caught up with my heart. "Bill, thank you. I should say I am sorry. You were only the catalyst for what needed to happen. I feel better now than I have in the last six weeks. You will never know how much this means to me to know that I can trust you, a man." His pained eyes vanished into confusion. I suddenly remembered that he did not know what had happened. *He will act different when he finds out. He won't be so kind.*

He did not know what I meant. Now I realized that I was not ready to move forward anymore today and I realized that I was going to have to trust that Bill would understand my silence. *I need his friendship right now. I don't have the right to use him like this but things will change soon enough when I tell him. But, I can't tell him what happened. Not now. Not yet. I can't even tell my family. How can I tell Bill.* A thought came to me and hoping that he would understand I said "Bill, I know you don't know what I mean right now but trust me. Besides, I'm hungry and was wondering if you would like to share a Hershey's chocolate bar with me. You don't have any feathers on you do you?"

Confusion deepened and then slowly transformed into laughter. "Sheryl, I don't understand what has happened here but right now I can't imagine anything that I could do that would make me happier than to spend more time with you. Come on! I owe you one don't I?" He flourished his arm and offered it to me. As I took it and we started down the hall I heard children. They were laughing, crying, and jumping with joy. I stopped, letting go of Bill's arm, and looked around for the school group that had to be visiting the University. I couldn't see the children anywhere. Shrugging my shoulders I decided that I had imagined the whole thing. I skipped the few steps that it took for me to catch up with Bill as we walked down the hall of the Ezra Taft Benson Chemistry Building. "Actually, Bill , it's my turn this time. You gave me one for Christmas, remember." As we stepped outside I looked up and thought. *Why haven't I noticed how beautiful the weather is. Thank you Heavenly Father.*

....

Sheryl's behavior confused me. What had she meant "... *I can trust you, a man.*"? I had seen her shudder a little as she pronounced the word *man*. She was not the person I had taken to Colorado. Something had happened since then, something that wasn't good. For a brief moment I wanted to rage at whatever had hurt her so much. The woman I knew seemed buried deep within this shell of a frightened girl. Even her clothing was drab and dark as if she wanted to just disappear into the woodwork and never be noticed. I sensed that she had been deeply hurt and that feeling made me want to break something. I clenched my fists as I looked around for David. For some reason I wanted to take a part of him and toss it through the window. My rage vanished as a calming feeling came over me and a voice tickled the back of my mind *"Daddy, just hold her. Give her time. You will see. Mom can deal with it. She needs you now."* I replied, *"Thanks Sophie. I'll try and remember that."* I paused for a moment to think. *Bill, you can't start talking to the voices in your head. It could be dangerous if they talk back!* For a moment I pictured her and Thomas jumping and dancing around us in a merry show of childish joy. Sophie was skipping and singing. *"I have a family there on earth ..."* I smiled at her antics and replied as Sheryl skipped forward to take my arm. "You are so like your mom." I didn't realize that I had spoken out loud until Sheryl replied.

"Thanks, Mom is the best person I know." As I led her out of the chemistry building I noticed that it was a beautiful spring day, warm with a gentle breeze smelling of new life and growth.

12

I completely forgot about Cindi and the past couple of months as Bill and I sat in the student center eating our chocolate. We laughed and remembered our trip. The people sitting next to us quietly got up and moved to another table. A few minutes later, another couple sat down only to move again. We didn't care. We were having too much fun. Occasionally Bill would reach across the table and take my hand in his to emphasize a point. My heart would jump each time he would do that and slowly my mind settled down and for the first time in what seemed like forever. I relaxed. It even seemed natural to accept Bill's offer to walk me home.

The closer we go to my apartment though, the more nervous I got as I thought about what was about to happen. *Ok Sheryl. Wonderland is over. It is time to wake up. This is a guy. A nice guy , but he is still a guy. You aren't worthy of him and you certainly can't invite him into your apartment. You don't have to imagine what will happen. You know. Besides he thinks you are the same girl he talked with and traveled with to Colorado. You aren't, you are below him. He will be gone as soon as he finds out about you. Don't hurt him by doing this. If you care about him at all cut the strings now.* My mind overrode my heart and I started to shake and sweat.

Bill noticed that something was wrong and stopped to allow me to compose myself. "Are you ok Sheryl?"

"I, I ... don't know... I ... yes I am but ... C-could you just let me go on from here?" *Don't let him go. But... Ignore that other voice. Follow your heart.* I was completely confused now. "I can make it from here."

"Sure no problem, but are you sure? You look a little ill." Just as he finished, Cindi walked up from behind him and broke the ice. Instantly my tremors ended.

"Hey Sheryl, how are you doing?"

"Oh! Hi Cindi, this is Bill. He was just taking me home." I tried to keep my face neutral as I fought the urge to rush over and give her a hug and say thank you for being there yet again. "Bill, this is Cindi, my roommate."

Cindi eyed Bill warily and stepped forward menacingly to stand between me and Bill. This, of course, looked funny. Bill was a foot taller than her and at least 50 pounds heavier. I started to laugh as I imagined a mouse standing up to a lion. Cindi realized that I wasn't feeling threatened any more and immediately smiled as she spoke. "He was? That's great. Thank you Bill." Thrusting her hand out to shake his she continued. "I don't think I have ever met you but since I am headed that way anyway why don't we all go together." She then took my arm in one hand and Bill's in the other and started us on the way.

She seemed oblivious to the fact that neither Bill nor I were saying anything. She was talking enough for all three of us. A few moments later we got home and Bill excused himself by saying that he was late for his workout and that he would call later that night. Cindi and I stood at the base of the stairs and watched him jog off. I breathed a sigh of relief as I realized that Bill was not going to come in after all. Then my heart jumped. *He is going to call tonight!*

It didn't take Cindi very much time to broach the subject. As soon as we closed the door she spoke. "Sheryl, are you ok. Bill wasn't a problem was he?" Her mothering me was nice but this time it was a little too stifling. I realized that Cindi was just concerned to have found me in a position that she and I knew that I could not have handled alone a week ago. I had to tell someone about my discoveries about myself and so I took Cindi in my arms and gave her a big hug and then led her into the living room where I told her about Bill.

As I told her of our trip to Colorado she sat patiently and smiled as I recalled the most memorable and fun parts about that trip. She started to cry as I told her about what had happened when I ran into Bill earlier in the day. She and I cried together when I told her what I had discovered about myself. I had another friend that I could trust almost as much as I trusted her. *At least until he finds out about me.* Cindi was not alone anymore.

"Sheryl, I don't know how you knew, but I needed a break today, when you came to me with the idea of trying to do your classes alone I nearly panicked. I didn't think you were ready for that but you seemed persistent and I decided to use this as my break. All day I have been praying that you would be ok. Then, when I was coming home just a few minutes ago I saw you on the verge of an emotional breakdown and I feared the worst. Instead I find that you have jumped so far forward into a new life that I can't help but feel that the Lord has heard my prayers." She gave me a big hug and then in a slightly teasing voice she continued. "You know that since you have made this big step, there is another that you can take that is just as safe and even more healing." A little scared and confused I just looked at her.

"There is one other person, like Bill, that you need to talk with. I know that Bishop Thomas has a free appointment this evening. If I went with you, would you feel comfortable talking with him now?"

For a moment I tensed with panic. Then my mind, which had matured and healed significantly with its experience with Bill earlier, took over. *I do need to talk with him. Maybe he can help me. Dr. Smithson even thinks so. Besides Cindi will be there so I guess that I could try it. He already knows what kind of a girl I am. I guess it's time to take one more step.* Slowly I nodded that I would go with her. She began crying again as she gave me another hug. "Sheryl, you are coming back to us. Now I know that the Lord answers prayers."

Later that evening as Cindi and I sat in the hallway outside of Bishop Thomas' office I had begun to rethink my earlier decision. *I can't do this. I shouldn't even be here. I have to go. Besides Bill was going to call and I have to be home or I will miss him.* Cindi held my hand and gave me the strength to face Bishop Thomas. As his office door opened to allow his earlier appointment to leave, the look on Bishop Thomas' face when he saw me sitting there took away all of my fear.

He looked at me through a mist of tears and spreading his arms wide to indicate that it was my turn and that I should precede him into the office. He spoke. "Sheryl, I was expecting Cindi. I am humbled to see you here. Would you feel more comfortable if Cindi joined us or would you like to talk privately."

"I think that I would like to talk privately." He looked past me to Cindi and acknowledged her part in getting me to finally come. "I need to talk to you alone."

His eyes misted over even more as he replied "Then please make your self at home here in my office while I go and make sure that we have all the time that we need." He went to the next office and knocked quietly. Shortly his executive secretary opened the door and they exchanged a few words and then he returned to close the door behind him. As he moved around the desk and sat down he spoke. "I have canceled the rest of my evening appointments so that we can talk for as long as you need to. I was just about to call and see how you were doing and now I am humbled to see you call on me. Would you mind if we started with a word of prayer? The Lord's spirit is here now but we need to express our gratitude before we continue."

We spent nearly two hours talking. I told him about my feelings of insecurity and guilt and how I was not sure that I would ever feel completely free of the evil thoughts that I had toward David. He assured me that I was not at fault and that there was nothing that I needed to feel guilty about. I told him about the conflicting voices in my head and how I was trying to heal but the voices kept confusing me. I told him that I knew that I was washed up and no good for anyone else. He just listened with tears running down his face and dripping onto his silk tie.

When I couldn't think of anything else to say he leaned forward across the desk and said. "Sheryl, you are a daughter of God. You Heavenly Father wants you to be happy. Do you think he would put those thoughts into your head? I don't. I know one other person who would though. Satan. He wants you to be miserable and to blame yourself for what happened. He wants you to never be happy and feel worthy to love another again. He wants you for himself. He is going to use these evil thoughts to grind you down until you are his.

You are stronger than him. You also have the right to the Holy Ghost to help you. You can triumph with God's help I know it. Pray to see if Heavenly Father really thinks these things about you. I promise that you will get an answer. I also promise that his answer will be that he still loves you and that your thoughts and fears are not from him."

He asked me a few questions about the temple and about my testimony. We talked about the gospel and the atonement of Jesus Christ. He offered to give me a blessing to ask the Lord to help me to understand the atonement and the principle of forgiveness better and to help me to be able to work out my feelings and thoughts. I accepted.

After he blessed me, we talked some more. I told him about Bill and how we had met. I told him that I thought Bill had been sent today as an answer to my prayers. He bore his testimony of the power of prayer and the interest that the Lord has in our lives and asked me to pray about the things we had talked about, especially the feelings that I had been having. I told him I would and agreed to come back in a week for another appointment. Before he would let me go, he pulled a pad out of his desk and wrote a few things in it. Turning the pad so that I could see it he asked me to sign the portion of the pad that he had been writing on. I hesitated and then spoke.

"Bishop, this is a Temple recommend. I am not worthy to go to the temple. I told you that."

He replied with tears in his eyes. "Sheryl, we have talked for two hours and in that time I have interviewed you about the temple and your worthiness to go there. Other than your ill feelings about David and what happened, you are worthy, in every way, to go to the Temple, more so than many others that I see. I feel strongly that the next level of healing that you will go through will be in the House of the Lord. You will need this."

"It will still need to be signed by the Stake President before you can use it. Take it, pray about it, think about the blessings that await you and then, when you are ready, make an appointment with President Mills."

I nodded assent and signed my recommend before rising. When we opened the door, Cindi was there waiting. Cindi and I talked excitedly about the new feelings that I was experiencing as we walked home.

There were flowers, yellow daisies - my favorite, and a card waiting for me when we arrived. The card read *"Sheryl, I don't know a better way to tell you just how much our time together today has meant to me. Daisies for the bright sunshine you have let into my life today. Sunshine where there has been darkness for many months. I don't know if there is more in the future (I can hope there is) but I want you to know that I will always be there for you, Your friend, Bill."* Excitedly I set about the kitchen with more energy than Cindi had ever seen from me. The flowers needed water and a vase before they could be placed on the table with just the right swatch of cloth under them.

He called a few minutes later to see if I had received them. We agreed to meet again the next day at the chemistry building. That night I didn't have any nightmares. Instead, I awoke blushing at the dream that came instead. Bill and I had been walking through a park, each of us pushing a stroller.

For the next few weeks I felt as though I was liberated. Bill and I spent more time together and Cindi and I spent less. Bishop Thomas and Dr. Smithson both upgraded me from critical to stable condition and our weekly interviews became every other week. The intensity of my feelings of inadequacy

216

and unworthiness decreased to a manageable level and there were some days when I didn't even have them at all.

Classes came to and end and I prepared for finals and graduation. I still had not told my parents, nor had I told Bill what had happened. Every night I would look at the Temple recommend sitting on my dresser and wonder *am I ready for this? Is it time? How will I know? When will I have to tell Bill or my family? What if they are repulsed by me? What if Bill never wants to see me again?* Before falling asleep I would read the scriptures and ask my Father in Heaven if he could help me continue to progress and to be healed.

One night, just before graduation, I dreamt that I was in a room filled with light. In through a door came a messenger dressed in white robes. He paused in front of me hovering somehow about a foot above the floor. He spoke. His voice sounded like a symphony of perfectly tuned instruments in the hands of master musicians.

"Father will see you shortly. You have time to speak with one visitor before I am to escort you through the veil to your new home. You will not see any of your earthly friends for some time after this. Not until it is their turn to see Father. Who would you like to see?"

A little stunned I replied. *"I don't know ..."* I was frightened at needing to make such a choice. *"... I love them all. They are all so important to me."*

"I know." The messenger said and then in a tender and loving voice he continued. *"That is why you will see them all again. But now you must choose. Will it be your Mother or Father? Or would you like to choose someone else?"* My mind quickly

began prioritizing my friends and family in a list. Who should I choose? Who is the most important to me? Mom? Dad? Cindi? Bill? Bishop Thomas? Even before I realized it the messenger was gone but not before saying *"A wise choice..."* Then I woke up.

I tried to remember who I had chosen. I couldn't . The following night I dreamt the same thing. When I woke up I decided I needed to pray. As I finished my prayer I had a strong feeling that Bill needed to know what had happened. I swallowed hard and decided I would tell him tonight after Family Home Evening.

....

I was happy. I was more than happy. Sheryl had been slowly returning to the bubbly and outgoing person that I had known in December. She never spoke about what happened but I knew that she would eventually. I had tried once to talk with Cindi about it but she told me that until Sheryl felt ready to tell me that it wasn't her right to do so. She did hint that it had not been easy for Sheryl and that I would need to be understanding when Sheryl finally told me. This worried me. What could possibly have happened?

It was the Monday before graduation when Sheryl finally decided that she needed to tell me. I had invited her to go to family home evening with me and she had accepted but when we got there she suddenly got very nervous and asked to leave. I asked if something was wrong but when she did not volunteer an answer and so I quickly escorted her out of the room. We decided to go for a walk instead.

As we wandered through the campus past the library and toward the art museum we were silent. Sheryl seemed to be cold because she shivered every once and a while as we walked. I reached over and put my arm around her shoulders and pulled her closer. That seemed to help because she didn't quiver nearly as much in the warm spring breeze. A few minutes later Sheryl stopped at a bench in the sculpture garden and sat down with her hands crossed in her lap.

After a few minutes she hesitantly began to speak. "Bill, I want you to know how much you mean to me. A month ago I was ready to kill my self and now I can't imagine such a thing. It was seeing you and feeling you in my life that has changed things." I was shocked. How bad was it. The Sheryl that I knew earlier would not have thought to do such a thing. My knees went week and I had to sit down. Reaching over I took her hands in mine as she continued. "I did not think that I had anything or anyone in my life worth living for." She stopped and looked up at me, her brown eyes painfully glistening in the evening light. "I was wrong. I had Cindi and, though I didn't know it, I had you. In some ways I am afraid that tomorrow, or even later tonight, I will revert back and feel the same way, especially after you hear this. I wouldn't blame you if you decided to leave in a few minutes. Before I go on I need to tell you that you have become the most important person in my life right now. I realized that last night and in a few minutes you will realize just how much that means and how much things have changed for me in the last few weeks."

My heart leapt into my throat at hearing how she felt about me. I wanted to say something but her eyes swallowed my words before they made it to my vocal chords. Instead I put my arm around her and pulled her closer. It wasn't long though before my heart began to break at what she was saying. She described the confusion and the pain. She told me that she didn't know for sure who had been the one to hurt her but that David had certainly been a factor in what had happened. She told me about sitting alone in her kitchen begging her arm to reach for the cooking knives and crying when her own body would not respond. She told me of the time that she did take an extra dose of her tranquilizer thinking that it would be enough to end things. Thankfully it wasn't.

Sheryl cried anew as she described the evil feelings and feelings of impotence that still wash over her from time to time. We both cried when she told me about how terrified she had been earlier as we had gone into family home evening to find that there were only two other girls present in the fourteen people there. I began shivering when I remembered the feelings that I had when I first met David. I sobbed to think that perhaps I could have saved Sheryl from having to go through this. I felt guilty. *I knew that David was no good and I hadn't done anything.* This thought tormented me. All I could do was hold her and cry for her.

After a few minutes I realized that Sheryl was dabbing at the tears on my cheeks and that I was the only one crying. I suddenly felt foolish and then I felt angry. I clenched my fists and through gritted teeth spoke. "Sheryl, where is he now? I have a few things I want to share with him. I have a few thoughts that I think he needs to have welded to his teeth." The last thing I expected to hear was her defending him.

Sighing deeply, Sheryl spoke. "Bill, please, getting angry doesn't help... I know. I spent too much time getting angry and it nearly killed me. I need you now. Besides, David is in jail, being punished, for giving me the drug. God will punish him for the rest of it. Besides, anger doesn't suit you."

"But Sheryl, he is slime."

"Yes he might be, but he is the Lord's slime and we will let Him decide how to deal with David. We ... No ... I need to move on. David has taken too much from me for me to allow him anymore of my time."

"I hear what you are saying. I don't know if my heart will listen though." After a few moments I continued. "How is it that you can forgive and defend him like that."

Sheryl's eyes bulged with surprise. She stuttered and sputtered as if in the midst of a seizure "I, I haven't forgiven him." Suddenly she jumped up and started walking. I ran to catch up with her. She started running.

In trying to keep up with her I was grateful that I had learned how to run and talk at the same time while exercising with Teri. "I'm sorry Sheryl for what I said. My heart has been yours since Christmas and it broke when I heard what you said. It was my pain speaking. Please understand." She didn't say anything. Instead she ran faster.

I reached for her hand in an effort to slow her down. She pulled it away and buried her face in her hands as she shuddered to a stop gasping through her sobs. "I haven't forgiven him! I will never forgive him! I hate him!"

I started to speak and then I realized that she wasn't talking to me. She was talking to herself and seemed to be trying to convince herself of something. I decided that I would wait for her to work out whatever it was that she was dealing with. Gently taking her hand away from her face, I held it tightly as we resumed walking.

The sun was just setting over the mountains to the west and the clouds were a bright orange as we turned north on 9th east. After a few minutes we neared the MTC. Sheryl had started to calm down as I saw the Temple lights blink on illuminating the solitary spire in an ethereal glow. Sheryl must have seen them too because she stopped and with her hand over her mouth in awe, she stared at the Temple as if transfixed in some kind of vision.

Slowly, with great effort, she started to speak. "Bill, I am sorry. I have spent months now convincing myself that I hated David and that I could never forgive him. Suddenly, when you said what you did I realized that I didn't hate him. I pity him and hate what he has done but I don't hate him. The realization shocked me." She reached over with her other hand and grasped my arm as she pulled herself closer, cuddling my right arm as she gazed at the spire, now glowing in the evening dusk. A few minutes later she continued. "It is so beautiful isn't it."

Her sudden change in topic was a little unnerving but it disarmed my earlier rage and I felt an overwhelming feeling of love and tenderness for her. I knew that someday I would ask her to go inside with me. As I thought about it I decided that I couldn't wait. "Sheryl, it is beautiful. I was going to go Wednesday after my last final. Would you go with me?" Her grip on my arm tightened for moment and then she nodded.

"I have to see President Mills first to get my recommend signed and then I can only do baptisms because I have not been endowed yet."

"I know." I leaned over and kissed the top of her head and then, as an after thought, I continued "Someday though, you will and I would like to be there when you are."

Sheryl replied "I want you there too. Thanks for understanding Bill. If you can still accept me after what I told you then I think my parents will. I still need to tell them. I think I can bring myself to do it now. They are coming on Wednesday night for graduation. Could you come over that night for dinner and be with me when I tell them?" She shuddered as she finished in a whisper that I am sure the slight breeze would have had trouble hearing.

"Sheryl, If you want me to, then I will. I don't think that you will have to worry about your parents though. I have never met finer people, your mother especially."

With a wistful smile she replied. "She is the best isn't she?"

"No Sheryl." She turned and looked into my eyes as we stood there under a street lamp. Her hair was pulled back in a scrunchy and her mascara had run down her cheeks. "You are the best. You are the most beautiful and the best." Her chin quivered as she digested what I had just said.

I wasn't aware that I was falling into her deep brown eyes until our lips met, first tentatively, and then with conviction as her arms reached up to my shoulders and she pulled me closer. After a few moments we turned and, holding hands, went home.

13

I was enraged at what David had visited on Sheryl. The woman I loved. I had come to the sudden realization Monday night that I did love Sheryl and that no matter what, I was going to be there for her. I also wanted to be there for David in a very different way. I was practically choking on my hate of him after I left Sheryl at her door Monday night.

I couldn't sleep at all. My mind kept running through scenarios where I would run into David somehow. I would hurt him and tell him to never touch Sheryl again. One scenario in particular enraged me so much that I actually got up, dressed, and drove out to the county jail to be there just in case David was released before morning.

In my fantasy, I was walking down the street and ran into David coming out of a building. I grabbed him by the collar and lifted him with one hand off the ground and into the air so that he hung helplessly above my face. His eyes were filled with terror as I began to shake him and hit him with my free fist. With each blow I felt my anger strengthen. For some reason he didn't fight back. He didn't defend himself.

I spat on him and then tossed him like a rag doll into a tree where his clothing caught on a limb and he hung there suspended. Slowly he began to fall as the limb gradually ripped into his clothing and flesh from the weight of his body pulling him toward the ground. As he fell, I once again vented my rage at him and then I turned and walked away leaving him there, a crumpled heap.

I was so enraptured with replaying the scene in my mind that I didn't notice the County Sheriff's Deputy until he knocked on the car door.

"Son, can I help you?"

"Wha ..." I jumped and banged my knee against the steering wheel. "What?" I said as I massaged the injured knee. His hand was on his gun and I saw that the strap securing it in the holster was loose.

"I said, can I help you? What are you doing here at three in the morning?"

"I ..." Suddenly I was deeply embarrassed and disappointed in myself for the words and the kind of language that I had used in my fantasy. I knew that my earlier feelings were completely wrong. I decided that I shouldn't offend God any further by lying to the officer so I told him the truth. "I just found out that the girl I love was hurt deeply by one of your guests. I suppose that in someway I was assuring myself that he couldn't come out and do it again." Tears were streaming down my face now and I collapsed into the steering wheel shaking with remorse for the evil that I had imagined myself doing to David. I couldn't forgive him but I certainly couldn't hurt him either. The officer spoke.

"I don't know which of our distinguished guests you mean but if the look in your eyes as I came up to the car means anything then you came real close to being one of them your self. Be careful son. Let the law and the Lord deal with this." He patted my back and then continued. "You have too much to loose by giving in to your hate, especially so soon after being hurt. Go home and think things through first. You don't want to go in there." He jerked his thumb towards the fence lined with razor wire. "A place like that is the last place you want to be. Go home."

I nodded and as he turned to leave I noticed that his hand casually reached up to brush something from his cheek, a *piece of dust or something.* I continued to think things through as I drove back to my apartment. *How can I forgive David for what he has done to Sheryl? How can she forgive him? Where can I go for peace on this?*

When I got home I fell into a fitful sleep and then skipped breakfast to go take my P-chem final. I know that my eyes were red and puffy as I walked into the exam room. Teri noticed and, before the exam started, asked what was wrong. I couldn't tell her but somehow hearing the concern in her voice shifted something in me. I suddenly wanted to forgive David. *I can't ask Sheryl to love me and someday be my wife if I still harbor hate for someone in her past, someone that she has forgiven. It would only strain our relationship in the future. I need to deal with this before I hurt Sheryl myself through the fruits of my hate for David. Please Heavenly Father, help me. I need to start on the right foot, with Sheryl, united in our forgiveness of David. I can't do it myself.* I realized that since I had skipped breakfast that I in some ways had already begun a fast. I resolved to end that fast having forgiven David, with the Lord's help.

I didn't even know what had been on my final when I turned it in two hours later. I was the first to do so. Teri was next by a few moments. Outside the examination room she caught me just as I was getting on the elevator to go up to my office.

"Bill, something is bothering you? Are you sure that I can't help?"

I shook my head and thanked her anyway. She seemed to understand that I needed to be alone. "Well, if you change your mind. I am going to go running at three this afternoon. I will wait at the bottom of the stairs." I thanked her again and pressed the button to the 3rd floor as the doors of the elevator closed.

I found a quiet corner in the laboratory and opened my scriptures up to read. I needed some guidance and the only way I knew to get it was through the scriptures. I was reading in the New Testament of the account of Christ's trial and crucifixion when it happened.

Suddenly I was there. I watched as the centurions threw his tired and abused body against the cross as it lay on the ground. I saw the blood begin to flow from where his shoulder had rubbed against the rough wood as the soldiers positioned his body. Hundreds of onlookers taunted him and spat at him as he closed his eyes and sought solace in some inner part of his being.

For a moment, just before the first blow to the spike positioned in the palm of his hand, his eyes opened and he looked at me. I wanted to run forward and wrest the mallet from the hand of the Roman Captain but I couldn't move. My feet were frozen. I saw the pain increase two fold, a hundred fold, and then in ever increasing multiples as the mallet dropped and the spike bit into the beam beneath his hand. Then again and again the mallet fell.

They spared him no mercy as they spiked his feet and wrists and placed a crown of thorns upon his head. Using his own blood the Captain scribbled something on a small piece of cloth rent from the Lord's own garments and tacked that to the beam above his head.

Then as the Captain stepped back to view his work a bystander broke through the lines of soldiers holding the crowd back. The man ran forward, murder in his eyes, and kicked dirt onto the wounds closest to him. The soldiers laughed. The captain clapped him on the back and motioned that he should give the order. In a loud and angry voice the man commanded the soldiers to lift the tree and plant it in the pit that had already been dug.

As the heavy timber dropped into the hole I noticed that suddenly all had gone silent. With a thud the tree was planted and the fruit, the precious fruit, that hung there grimaced in increased pain. The voices of the crowd once again erupted and drowned out the weeping of a small group of onlookers standing off to one side.

Suddenly I saw myself as I had been earlier that morning. I saw myself as I had imagined meeting David. I heard myself as I raged at, beat, and spat upon him. I saw his pain and reveled in it. I witnessed as I scuffed dirt into David's eyes as he lay there, having fallen from the tree I had placed him in. Then my vision cleared as I looked once more on the man that hung before me.

His eyes had never left me. As the picture washed from before my eyes in a torrent of tears I heard the Savior say *"... forgive them for they know not what they do."*

I knelt there in the corner of my laboratory and wept. I had been the Commander, the crowd, and the man who had come forward to torment David. I had done so in my own mind but I felt as though I had done it none the same.

As my grief-weakened body slowly fell into a fitful sleep I mumbled to myself. "I must see past what David has done and forgive..."

When I awoke my knees were sore and my back was wrenched in a very uncomfortable angle from being there on the floor. I glanced at my watch and suddenly realized that it was ten o'clock at night. I had been there the whole afternoon. Grimacing as I started to stand I remembered the Savior's face as the cross fell into the hole dug in the rock to hold it. I heard Sophie's voice from my right. *"Dad ... if mom and the Savior can forgive him then so can you."*

Always, before, it had sounded as though her voice was coming from everywhere at once.

Curious, I looked to my right and saw Sophie and Thomas dressed in white. Each was holding the hand of an adult who was also dressed in white. The hands were scared and marked at the wrist and in the middle as if they had been perforated at some time in the past. I began to wonder and then hope, could it be? Even as I raised my eyes towards the face of the adult to assuage my increasing awe at the blessing I was a recipient of, the vision vanished but not without Sophie blowing me a kiss. *"We love you Dad."*

I walked home then, a new peace growing in my heart. I still had trouble with what David had done but I knew that if I ever did run into him on the street that I could let the opportunity pass without anger taking over. I had not fully forgiven him. I knew that. It would take time for that to come. I did know that I could forgive him and that gave me the strength that I needed.

14

Wednesday afternoon Sheryl and I went to the baptistry at the Temple and then, on our way to her apartment we stopped at the grocery store and got the ingredients for the spinach lasagna we were going to make for dinner. With the exception of the day before, I had never felt the spirit stronger than when I had been in the Temple with Sheryl.

I had intended to do some baptisms too but when we had arrived the baptistry supervisor asked if I would be a worker instead so I was in the font when Sheryl came in dressed in white to be baptized for sisters whose births and deaths had preceded the restoration of the gospel. Somehow I felt as though, with each name I baptized her for, I was washing Sheryl's traumatic past away replacing it with something cleaner, purer, more celestial. For me I felt increasingly free from the pain and evil feelings that I had for David with each performance of the ordinance. The Lord was showing me how to forgive David. I know Sheryl felt it too because as we left she whispered that she felt newly baptized herself.

Sheryl was nervous when her parents came to the door the next day. She had made arrangements with her roommates for them to be somewhere else. Cindi was the only exception. She joined us for dinner and then

afterwards she excused herself as Sheryl showed her parents to the living room.

I sensed that Sheryl wanted a few minutes alone with them so I offered to clear

the table. Sheryl hesitated a moment and, realizing what I was doing, smiled

and nodded through the tears that were beading up in the corners of her eyes. I

grabbed her hand for a moment and whispered that I would be there when she

needed me. *I will never go away Sheryl. I will always love you.*

A few moments later I heard her parents gasp and then Sheryl's mother

began to cry. Fighting the urge to look in on them I knelt there on the kitchen

floor and asked Heavenly Father to give Sheryl strength to trust her parents

with the whole truth. I begged Him to give them the wisdom to deal with what

would un-doubt ably be the most painful thing they would experience. I knew.

It had only been two days for me and I still was in shock with the reality of the

situation.

I was still on my knees when, nearly an hour later, they all came back

into the kitchen. The dishes were still on the table and the food was still not

put away but it didn't matter. For the rest of the night, as we all cried and

comforted each other, we grew closer and in some part began to realize just

how much our Heavenly Father loved each of us.

Sheryl graduated the next morning and we all celebrated by going

shopping. Sheryl had decided that she needed a new wardrobe to go with her new job. She would be working for the Deseret News as a Utah county reporter.

Sheryl's mom agreed. I did my part keeping Sheryl's dad company through the long hours of following them around. A couple hours into our spree Sheryl's dad and I were alone waiting for the girls who where in the dressing room trying on some dress suits for interviews. He hesitantly broached the subject that we had successfully avoided so far for most of the day.

"Bill, she has changed hasn't she?" Swallowing hard I nodded. "Once again you have come through. You have been there when my princess needed you." His voice faltered and he took a few moments before he continued. "She is still the jewel of my eye and I see that, though she is still tender in many ways, she has been refined and someday she will shine even brighter than she did before. Thank you for being there for her when she needed you. I don't know how to ever show you just how much that means to me so please just accept my gratitude."

I replied, "Paul, Sheryl is a wonder to me. I know that I don't have the strength to have gone through what she did. I have never prayed more than I have in the last couple of days since I learned what it was that had changed her so much and I know that it has taxed what little strength and faith that I do have. She is the one that seems to be supporting me right now. It is amazing. She has already forgiven David. I still wake up shaking from thinking about what I might do if I ever met him again."

Sheryl's father nodded briefly before looking away with a deep sadness in his eyes. "I know Bill. I know. I couldn't sleep last night because I was so worked up. I was ready to forsake all I know to be correct to avenge her. It was Mary that helped me to realize that our duty was to support Sheryl in her decisions and if she forgave David then we had to do so as well. I am humbled by the spiritual giant that I see coming to maturity in my daughter. I see in her the very same qualities I saw in Mary thirty-eight years ago."

"I know what you mean." I told him about my experience a couple of days before, everything except Sophie and Thomas. "It scares me when I look at myself and see the child that I am."

"You have what it takes though Bill. You are well on your own way toward forgiving him."

"Thanks. I know. The Lord has helped out a lot among other things." I was thinking of Sophie and Thomas. They had helped me too.

"You also have more than you know. You have her heart. Sheryl loves you. Mary and I can tell. Sheryl doesn't know it yet but when she does, watch out. When that time comes, you have Mary's and my support."

I had the tears now as I reached for Paul's hand and pulled him into an embrace. "Thank you. I love her too. I will be ready when she learns and understands that she has mine. I am not going anywhere until she does."

Last – Chocolat

"Sheryl dear, weren't the Christmas lights beautiful as we came in? The trees were perfectly trimmed too."

Mom was helping me to put my veil on. Bill's mother had left us alone in the Bride's dressing room a few moments earlier to join her husband in the sealing room. In a few minutes Bill and I were going to be married. As Mom fussed with a particularly unruly curl that didn't want to stay in my headpiece, I could not help but to remember that night years ago when Mom and Dad had pulled me and my brother Thomas aside to tell us that she and Dad had planned a special family-home-evening and that we were expected to be available the next evening to participate in it. Even now I wonder what ever made my mom think of such a lesson.

"Yes mom. They are part of what will make today perfect too." I said as I turned to look at her instead of watching her in the mirror. I continued a little more tenderly "Mom?"

"Yes Pum'kin." She replied a little absent mindedly.

"Do you remember that family-home-evening we had years ago?"

Mom's already misty eyes filled again and in a whisper she replied, "Yes Sheryl. I remember it. In fact I was just thinking of that. Your father and I knew this day would come and we wanted you to be prepared to meet it with your whole heart and soul. Being married in the Temple is not a simple thing. It takes preparation, even years in advance, to be worthy."

My eyes were misty now. I swallowed hard and then took a deep breath. It would not be good for me to mess up my mascara with only ten minutes left before I got married. Somehow the deep breath only served to make my voice more husky as I hurried on with what I wanted to say.

"You told me something on the telephone just before Bill and I started out driving to Colorado for Christmas. You told me that I should remember to bring you a chocolate bar – I remember I brought you your favorite – a *Snickers* bar." I was close to tears now and I paused to compose myself before continuing. "I thought at the time that you were crazy. I remembered the significance of the chocolate bar but I did not see that there would ever be a need for it with Bill. By the time I got home the next afternoon because of the road closure, I had come to realize that you may not have been so crazy after all. Now I know you weren't."

Mom was in tears now. Before she could say anything and cause me to start crying I continued. "I love Bill, I think that I always have. David distracted me for a little while but something in me recognized Bill when I first saw him. I had chosen to suppress and deny those feelings because of David. Your comment on the phone only got me to thinking and then ..." I was crying now and I did not care! As I tried to focus on mom's face through my tears, I reached out to hug her.

"Thank you for believing in me and accepting me, mistakes and all. I don't know what I would have done if you and Dad had turned away from me after last winter. I love you mom. You always knew when I would need a little of your wisdom even when I refused to take it. Thanks."

"I know honey, I know. We couldn't turn from you when you needed us and we never will."

"In about five minutes I will be married to my Mr. Right, the man that you and dad somehow new would come along when you gave Thomas and I that lesson. I will become Mrs. Wright. Before we go into the sealing room, I want you to have something from me to say thanks for our talks, your wisdom, and your lectures over the years."

Reaching into my travel case, I pulled out the small package that I had secreted away the night before. I had wrapped it in gold foil and tied it with a red bow. "Mom," My voice broke and I swallowed hard, "here is my chocolate bar. It is untouched and perfect."

Mom's arms nearly crushed me with her hug. I had never realized that mom could muster so much strength. In her own broken voice she replied, "I have some thing for you too Pum'kin." Reaching into her purse she withdrew a monster size chocolate bar with a red bow taped to the end and handed it to me. "Eight years ago we promised to trade on this day. I am so happy to know that we can. This is for you and Bill. Enjoy it, savor it, and then share the lessons that you learn from it with your own children."

......

It was late now. The sealing room had been packed with friends and loved ones. Bill's father nearly had us all crying with his sentiment as distorted as it was due to his earlier stroke. Later at the reception, people I hardly knew congratulated us on our choice. Bill and I had left after the last of the guests had filed through our reception line.

Bill was in the bathroom now, changing into his pajamas. He had let me change earlier. Knowing that now was the time to let Bill know the answer to a question he had asked months before, I placed the chocolate bar that mom had given me on his pillow as I waited for him to join me in our bed.

He came out shyly and quietly looked at me, my back propped up with pillows as I waited to give him my chocolate. "I love you Sheryl. I always have."

"I know Bill, but I owe you something for your patience with me. Do you remember when we were trapped in Vail with that snow storm? We were hungry and all of the stores were sold out of food."

"Yes I remember, You had a *Snickers* bar in your purse but you refused to open it so that we could eat something. You were importing it from Utah for your mother."

"I was so hungry then and I was so tempted to open it and eat it with you but I knew something that you did not know and I want you to understand that now. You see that *Snickers* bar was not just any chocolate bar. It was symbolic to me just like this one here on your pillow."

This was the first time that Bill had noticed the candy bar. Confusion rolled through his eyes. "Why is there a chocolate bar on my pillow?"

"Years ago mom and dad held a special family-home-evening with Thomas and I." I patted the bed beside me, indicating that I wanted to have him next to me. Bill lifted the candy bar from his pillow and crawled under the blankets with me. I scooted closer and cuddled up next to him before continuing. We held hands as we gazed at the candy bar now sitting on the comforter before us.

"The family-home-evening was on preparing for a temple marriage. As we listened and they talked, they unwrapped two chocolate bars and placed them on plates in front of us. We discussed the Temple and temple marriage and the choices that we could make that could keep us from being able and worthy to attend the Temple. As each possible barrier to a temple marriage was discussed, they mutilated one of the chocolate bars leaving the other untouched. When the lesson was over, they asked us which candy bar we would like to eat.

We looked at the crumbly, half-melted, mass of nuts and caramel and whatever that had once been a pristine candy bar and then we looked at the perfect, unblemished bar. We decided that we wanted to have that one."

"Mom and Dad pointed out that we, Thomas and I, along with our future spouses, were the chocoate bars and just like we wanted the perfect ones for ourselves so would our future spouse. Mom and Dad then gave us each a chocolate bar and told us that it was our own and that we could do whatever we wanted with it and that they would always love us no matter what we chose to do with it, but if we could keep it clean and pristine and return it to them on the day of our wedding in the temple that they would guarantee us the best and most beautiful day of our lives." I paused before continuing.

"Of course the candy bar was only symbolic and Thomas and I ate ours within days of getting them from Mom and Dad but we never forgot the lesson and every time we would return home from a long trip or absence we would bring with us a new chocolate bar as a sign to Mom and Dad that we still remembered the lesson and still had as our goal a Temple marriage."

"For a long time after David drugged me I thought that my life had been destroyed like the mutilated candy bar in the lesson. You, Cindi, Bishop Thomas, and Dr. Smithson helped me to realize that I hadn't made those choices and so I still had a perfect love and heart to offer. Here it is Bill." I turned to look into his eyes. "Here is my chocolate bar. I want you to share it with me now. It is unblemished and worthy of you."

Recognition and understanding flooded Bills eyes. Then, through tears, he mumbled. I had thought that Bill had been holding me close but the hug he gave me corrected that thought. I thought I had cried enough but Bill's sudden tenderness overwhelmed me. After a very long time I pushed him away so that I could look into his eyes once more. I saw heaven mirrored there.

Bill hesitated, looking at the candy bar before us, and then with tears in his eyes he said; "Sheryl, I am so grateful that you did not share your chocolate bar with me that night in Vail. Somehow I think this chocolate will fill us up in more ways than that other one ever could have." With a slight smile he continued. "You know I really did do a scientific study. I decided that the Utah chocolate bars when imported to Colorado really do taste better."

My voice failed me as my throat choked up with emotion. Instead of saying anything, I cuddled up next to my new-made husband, he lifted our candy bar from the blanket before us. Opening it, we looked at it one last time before taking our first tentative bites. As I rolled the caramel and chocolate around in my mouth, I seemed to hear children running and laughing in my head. Then voices yelling *"Mommy's going to be It. We are going to get you mommy!"*

Surprised at the voices I asked, "Did you hear that?"

"Hear what?"

"Voices ... children's voices."

Bill smiled, swallowed, and then said "Pum'kin I've been hearing those voices ever since we bumped heads that night at your front door. I'm just not so sure if they bode good or ill for our future." I looked at him in what must have been confusion. He smiled again, kissed my forehead and then continued. "There are two of them you know."

I knew I could be happy but I never imagined that I could be this happy.

www.ingramcontent.com/pod-product-compliance
Lightning Source LLC
Chambersburg PA
CBHW020831260626
47169CB00003B/927